# THE SWORDSMAN'S INTENT

A ROYAL CHAMPION NOVELLA

G.M. WHITE

TWIN STAR PRESS

The Swordsman's Intent
G.M. White


Editor: Vicky Brewster
Cover design: Get Covers

# AUTHOR'S NOTE ON SPELLINGS
# (AND AI)

Please note, the author is British, and so uses British English spellings throughout.

No AI was used in the writing of this book, it is the work of a human mind with all the frailties and faults that entails.

1

Ervan looked at the invitation that one of the staff had just handed him. The wax that sealed it had been pressed into two crossed swords, the crest of Markus, the Royal Champion of Villan, defender of the king's honour. His hands had a slight tremble to them as he opened the envelope.

"Well, what is it?" his mother, Lavinia, asked from behind her teacup. They were sat in one of the most luxuriously appointed parlours in their home, chosen by his mother for the midmorning light that came in through the windows. She found it particularly alluring at this time of year. They had been sitting down to tea when the servant knocked gently on the door before delivering up his missive.

Ervan's eyes scanned the contents of the envelope, a slight frown resting on his brow. He was a handsome young man in his early twenties, dressed in what some deemed to be the overly foppish fashions popular at court this year. His sandy blond hair was cut rakishly long, his black doublet slashed with red velvet and trimmed with large quantities of lace at the neck and wrists. Despite his good looks, there was a coldness to his gaze that no one could quite thaw.

"It's an invitation."

"I can see that. From the Royal Champion himself, unless my eyes deceive me. But to what?" His mother was a handsome woman, her black hair only faintly laced with silver, her face almost unlined, but her eyes held a similar chill to Ervan's. She dressed more modestly, in the fashions of the previous generation: a high-cut gown with elaborately embroidered panels, scarlet foxes chasing each other across her décolletage.

"To train. With him and some other specially selected students."

"He can't have failed to notice your talent with a blade. You've won every fencing competition worth note in the city. Perhaps..."

Ervan looked up at his mother. "Perhaps what?"

"He's not getting any younger. Perhaps he's looking for his replacement."

A slow smile crept across Ervan's face. "Perhaps he is."

Lavinia sniffed. "Then perhaps all those expensive fencing lessons were worth it." A smile took a little of the bite from her words.

Belasko ducked under the tent flap, preparing himself for a meeting with his superior officer—who was not always the easiest person to read.

She sat behind a small writing desk, her silver hair gleaming in the lamplight. She smiled, the glimmer in her eyes undimmed by age. "You're going up in the world," General Zakian said. "I have a letter here asking for your release from your commission so you can attend some training."

Belasko swallowed. "Training? What sort of training?"

"That's the thing. It's not terribly clear." She frowned. "I'm guessing, as it came from Markus, our esteemed Royal Champion, that it's something to do with swordplay." She stopped, softening for a moment. "You're a damn fine swordsman, Belasko. You do the army proud, so I suppose it's only right you be summoned. Although you'll be difficult to replace."

"Summoned?" Belasko frowned. "Summoned to what?"

General Zakian sat back in her chair, picking up the envelope that contained the only clue to Belasko's immediate future and tapping it on the desk. She paused, a thoughtful look on her face, before arriving at a conclusion. She nodded to herself. "Yes, that must be it." She sat up straighter. "Markus isn't a young man anymore. I hear word that he's looking to step down. He may be looking for his replacement."

"As Royal Champion? And he wants me?"

She laughed. "Don't go getting ahead of yourself, Belasko. From the way they phrase this letter, I warrant you'll not be the only one in attendance. You'll likely have to prove yourself against the finest blades in the kingdom. Here, have a look for yourself." She tossed him the letter, which he snatched out of the air, removed from its envelope, and quickly scanned its contents.

Belasko looked up at the General. "This says they request my presence next week."

General Zakian nodded. "That's right."

"But we're in the middle of training fresh recruits, finding places for them. I can't just leave."

"No, you can't. It would be a dereliction of duty, and I

know you're not a man who would skip out on his duties. So you'll be released, but not until your replacement arrives." She picked up another letter from her desk, waving it in the air. "As luck would have it, a replacement that has already been arranged. Hopefully, they'll arrive in time for you to be on your way and attend this training."

Belasko stood for a moment, uncertainty writ large across his face. "But I'm a soldier, not a fencer. I'm not going to fit in at all."

General Zakian stood, coming around from behind her desk to stand in front of Belasko. She grasped him by the shoulders. "Yes, you are a soldier, and a damn good one. More than that, you're a warrior born. The Royal Champion isn't just some toffee-nosed fencing school figure. They're the embodiment of the king's own honour, the country's honour, which they are called upon to defend from time to time. As I believe I've already said, you're a damn fine swordsman. Perhaps the best I've seen in a long time. Your feats during the war with the Baskans are already becoming legend. So go to this training. Show those society nitwits in Villan what a soldier is made of." She smiled. "Now get out of my tent. I have work to do."

Belasko left, going back to the tent he shared with his fellow officer and best friend, Orren. The big bear of a man stood up as Belasko entered, brushing back his shaggy blond hair that never seemed to be cut to regulation length. He handed Belasko a cup of wine that he had at the ready.

"What did the General want? New orders?"

Belasko took a long swallow of his wine. He drew the

back of his free hand across his lips and nodded. "Of a sort. For me, at least."

Orren frowned. "What do you mean?"

"My presence is requested by the Royal Champion to attend some training. General Zakian thinks he's looking to choose his successor."

"You?" Orren snorted. "A farmer's son, among all the high muckety mucks from those fancy fencing schools?"

Belasko sighed. "That's what I was thinking."

"Actually," Orren said, laughing, "I was thinking I'd love to see you dump them on their high and mighty arses. You're pretty handy with that pig sticker." He pointed at the army regulation arming sword scabbarded at Belasko's waist. "In fact, please tell them that's how you learned to use it. Chasing pigs around the farmyard."

Belasko laughed as well. "I might just do that." He drained his wine, which Orren refilled, topping up his own cup as well. "To think, I have a chance to become the next Royal Champion. That would be... I mean, the Royal Champion is acknowledged as the best blade in the kingdom. It's an amazing opportunity."

"Yes, to enjoy the wealth and privilege that goes along with it! You've come a long way from your parents' mountain farm. When do you leave? How long for?" Orren asked.

Belasko shrugged. "As soon as my replacement arrives, and I don't know. The letter they sent said nothing about how long I would be away."

"Don't forget you have an important engagement to be at next month." Orren pointed a meaty finger at Belasko. "You're to stand by me when I marry Denna. I wouldn't have anyone else by my side."

"How could I forget? Of course I'll be there. I'll explain if needs be. I'm sure they'll be understanding."

"Good. They'd better be!" Orren enveloped Belasko in a fierce bear hug. "I love you, my brother. I need you there when I wed Denna. It'll be the most important day of my life."

Belasko patted his best friend's back. "I love you too, brother." He managed to keep the sadness out of his voice.

They had gathered, these invited few, for this first day of... *What?* thought Ervan. *A fencing school?* The young noble looked around him, taking in the rag-tag bunch that were gathered. There were eighteen others apart from him, all fairly young—men, women, higher and lower class. Some were dressed in court finery, others in the uniforms of assorted branches of the Villanese military. The only unifying characteristic among them was that they all moved with the grace of experienced—or at least well-practised—swordsmen and women.

They had all been summoned to this place, a long low-ceilinged room in a former city watch barracks. The barracks itself was in a down at heel area just within the city's outer wall. It was now a little too antiquated for its intended purpose and was available for their use as the watch company in question had moved on to newer surroundings, and there was to be a short period before it was repurposed permanently.

Markus, the Royal Champion and the person who had convened this gathering, looked around, taking in those gathered. His forehead creased in a slight frown, then he shook his head and called for quiet. He was a tall man of wiry strength and deceptive speed, whose dark brown hair was thinning. Hair and beard were both shot through with grey, and he was quietly spoken. They all leaned in to listen.

"Thank you all for coming. I'm glad to see that you decided to attend. In fact, only one I invited is missing, which is better than I expected. So why did I ask you here? Well, I—"

Markus was interrupted as the door crashed open, admitting a soldier who was in something of a hurry.

"Sorry I'm late," the newcomer said. "I was only released from my commission yesterday. I rode through the night to get here." He was an unprepossessing fellow in appearance, Ervan thought. Slender and of average height, but again he moved well, and his travel-stained uniform showed that he was a Colonel. A lofty rank for one who wasn't much older than Ervan himself.

Markus smiled. "I'm glad you could join us. Come in and close the door after you. Where was I? Oh yes..."

Belasko closed the door gently behind him, staying near the back of the group as Markus continued his speech.

"... are all here because of your skill with a blade. I have been looking, for some time, to find my replacement. It is my belief that they stand here, in this room. I have always kept my eyes open for those gifted with a blade. Some of you I have seen fight with my own eyes; others I know only by reputation. The next few weeks will see if those reputations are deserved. I will put you through your paces. We will work and train alongside each other, and by the end of our time together, I hope I will have named my replacement, the one who will follow me as Royal Champion to the King of Villan."

A murmur ran around the room, and it surprised Belasko to find that he could feel his heart beating like a drum in his chest. Could he... could he be the next Champion?

"Now then," Markus said as they all quieted down, "while you all come from varied walks of life, you are all here as students. I don't care what your station is outside these doors. Here you are equals and will treat each other as such. Am I understood?" His new students looked around at each other, nodding and mumbling their assent. "I'm sorry, I didn't quite catch that." This time the students chorused their approval. Markus smiled. "Good. Now, over here, we have an array of training blades. Find one that suits you and let's begin."

Belasko wandered over to the rack of training blades, nodding to his fellow students as he caught their eye. Only one student didn't go to the rack, instead collecting a case set against the wall of the salon. He was a foppish looking young man, dressed in the latest fashions of court, which to Belasko's mind, involved far too much lace. The man shook his blond hair out of his eyes and undid the clasps on the case. He perused the contents, lips pursed, and eventually drew out a training blade of fine make: a rapier.

"Watching young master Ervan won't help you select your own blade." The voice sounded from over Belasko's shoulder, making him jump. He whirled around to find Markus stood just behind him, a gentle smile on his face taking any sting out of his words. "Here, let me help you."

Markus took Belasko's elbow and led him the rest of the way to the rack. "Now, let me see..." The older man stroked his beard in thought. "You've come up through the infantry, yes?" Belasko nodded. "You may be more used to a single-handed arming sword, but I think you'll find one of these more suitable for our work here. Yes, this one I'd say." Markus drew a training rapier from the rack and passed it to Belasko. "The length and weight should suit you, unless I've lost my eye. Here, try it for balance."

Belasko held the blade, feeling its balance as he tried out a few test slashes and thrusts, sending the blade whistling through the air as he did so. He nodded to himself before turning back to Markus. "Thank you," he said. "I have used a rapier before, usually alongside a dagger, but you haven't lost your eye. It's as if it were made for me."

"I'm glad to hear it, on both counts. The rapier is a duelist's weapon—light enough that it won't tire you too fast, but heavy enough to do some damage. Sharp enough normally, too, although these are blunted. Get more acquainted with her while I help some others find their blades." He patted Belasko on the shoulder before moving off toward another student dressed in cavalry uniform who was weighing a training sabre in her hands. "Ah yes, a suitable choice, but have you considered a shorter blade? You might find that a little unwieldy..."

Belasko moved into the centre of the room to warm up. While he had been talking to Markus, the young courtier who the Royal Champion had named as Ervan had been moving through a warm-up routine of his own. Belasko had to admit that he moved well, with a deadly grace that belied his foppish appearance. As Ervan turned towards him, Belasko caught his eye and nodded a greeting. The courtier's eyes met his with no accompanying look of recognition. Then the young man turned his back on Belasko.

Ervan ignored the peasant in the military uniform. Markus could make all the high minded speeches he liked. You couldn't deny the truth of Villanese society. He was different from most of these others—of noble blood, and he wouldn't forget it in a hurry. His family could trace their roots right back to the founding of the first city. What could he possibly have in common with these peasants?

Markus had finished helping others to select their blades. He moved back into the centre of the room and gestured them all to gather around. Ervan ceased his warm-up routine, placing his hands on the pommel of his training blade as he rested it point down on the floor. The Royal Champion began to speak.

"There are some among you, judging by your uniforms, who have already fought for the highest stakes: your lives. There are others here who are fresh from fencing acad-emies, who've yet to face an opponent with anything other than a practice blade. This is nothing to be ashamed of, but I'd like to get a measure of the experience in the room. So, put your hands up. You'll take them down again when called."

Everyone did as he asked, with a few sheepish glances among them.

"Now," Markus said, "lower your hand if you've only ever faced an opponent with a practice blade."

Ervan, faced flushed with embarrassment, took his hand down. He wasn't the only one, but quite a few hands remained raised.

Markus nodded. "Good—and there's no shame in that. We all start from somewhere. Now, who has faced an oppo-nent with live blades and fought to the death, not first blood?"

The only hands that remained belonged to members of the Villanese military.

"And who has fought in a duel?"

Only one hand stayed in the air. It belonged to the soldier who had arrived late.

"Which obviously you won, or you wouldn't be standing with us today." Markus smiled. "Would you care to tell the class where you fought your duel, and with whom?"

Quietly, so they had to strain to hear, the soldier said, "At Dellan pass. I fought the champion of the Baskan army."

A murmur ran around the room, and Ervan found himself staring at the soldier. This was Belasko, the great hero of the Last War? The one the troubadours sang of?

"We have some impressive reputations here with us. All of you have unique experience. And those with more will help those who are closer to the start of their journey. Let us begin."

First, Markus had them place their practice blades by their feet while he led them through some physical exercises, to "get the blood flowing". Then he had them work through some solo drills as he walked amongst them, correcting posture and stance here, a murmured word of advice there, before pairing them up to work through some drills and exercises together.

"To begin with, you'll work with people who are a close physical match in terms of height, reach, and so on. As we progress through the next few weeks, your partners will vary in order to present you with the greatest challenges and opportunities to stretch yourself. Today I am just trying to get a feel for your abilities, so please keep to the exercises as given. No extemporising."

Belasko found himself paired with the sandy-haired young courtier he had observed earlier, the one who had brought his own training blade. He offered the other student his hand.

"Belasko. Markus said your name was Ervan? Nice to meet you."

Ervan, with an expression of mild distaste that was not easily hidden, gave his hand a peremptory shake.

"No," said Belasko, "like this. If we're brothers in arms under Markus's tutelage, then we should use the warrior's grip." He slid his hand up above Ervan's wrist to hold his forearm, correcting the other man's grip on his own arm, before giving a more emphatic shake and releasing his hold.

The look of distaste on Ervan's face was no longer mild. "I'm not sure we could be considered brothers in anything. I'm not a soldier."

"Yes, your clothing does rather give that away. Although you must be skilled with a blade for Markus to invite you here; you must have something of the warrior about you."

Ervan sniffed. "Yes, well, I have won the city fencing championships for the last three years running, which Markus judged himself. He's aware of my quality."

"Is he now? That's good. Curious that he paired us together. Perhaps he thinks we have something to teach each other? Although I've never attended a fencing school, or anything so refined as a competition. What I've learned of handling a blade has come through my army training, practice, and my best efforts at staying alive. I'm sure your technique is... more refined."

"I don't doubt it. It will certainly be interesting to cross blades with the hero of Dellan Pass. I must get that story from your own lips. The version the balladeers sing of... it can't all be true."

Belasko smiled. "Let's just say they tell a more... exaggerated version of events. It's not something I like to dwell on. I might tell of it later. Meantime, we'd best follow Markus's instructions."

Markus had finished pairing up the other students as they'd been talking. He retook his place at the front of the room, picked up his own practice blade from the floor, and began to talk the students through an exercise.

Ervan gritted his teeth in frustration. Markus had set them simple exercises, basic stances, thrusts, parries, and ripostes—the simplicities covered in a beginners' fencing class. The level of ability in the room was far above such basics, but perhaps that was Markus's intention. Take them back to the fundamentals, see what they were made of. Although running through such beginners' exercises was annoying to Ervan, that was not why he was frustrated.

He had barely landed a touch on Belasko all morning. The soldier's technique was as rough and ready as his manner, but he was quick. Blindingly quick. He had landed as many strikes on Ervan as the young courtier had been able to dole out. They appeared to be equally matched, which was a victory for Belasko as far as Ervan was concerned. *I should be thrashing him. Instead, he's the equal of me. He doesn't even have the decency to be triumphant. He's being...* nice *about it.*

Belasko continued to smile, enjoying the exercises, encouraging Ervan—who found the whole thing infuriating. Markus called a break, and he wiped the sweat from his eyes as he stood back.

The Royal Champion gestured to a table set against one wall and laden with fresh fruit, bread, and cheese. "Time for some refreshments. Come and help yourselves. Don't take too much, mind. You don't want to make yourselves sick when we continue."

Belasko clapped Ervan on the shoulder. "Come on. I don't know about you, but I've worked up a bit of a thirst."

Ervan sighed but followed Belasko over to a water butt positioned at one end of the table. The soldier picked up a cup, dipping it into the barrel and sipping from it as he surveyed the spread. He turned to Ervan. "One thing a soldier learns: eat when food's available. Although not too much if action is expected. I'll take a few slices of that melon and an orange. Bread and cheese might be somewhat heavy."

"Coarse, too. Common food." Ervan sniffed. "Lead on. I'll follow your example."

Ervan leaned forward as they took up their place in the line, murmuring to Belasko, "Now, about Dellan Pass..."

The soldier grinned. "I wondered how long that would take. What would you like to know?"

"Well," Ervan frowned, "the story is that you held the pass on your own for an entire day, before challenging the Baskan champion to a duel to decide the battle. That can't be true. It's just not possible."

Belasko shrugged. "That's more or less what happened. If I learned one thing that day, it's that to achieve something people believe to be impossible, you have to keep working at what's in front of you—one task at a time. Whether you're building walls, digging ditches, or killing enemy soldiers, there's only one way to get a job done."

The rest of the students had quieted, eavesdropping on their conversation.

Ervan shook his head. "I can't believe it. You held the pass, on your own, for a whole day?"

Belasko nodded. "My friend Orren and I were dispatched to check the pass, to make sure the Baskans weren't moving through it—which no one thought was likely as it's so narrow at points that it's only possible to pass through in single file." Belasko picked up a plate, waiting to move forward in the line. "To our surprise, we found a large Baskan force at the other end of the pass. Orren was the better horseman, and I the better swordsman, so I sent him back to raise the alarm and return with our own forces while I held the pass as long as I could."

He moved forwards, picking up a slice of melon and putting it on his plate. "I had to hold the pass for all of the next day to give him time, which seemed impossible, but I did what I could." Belasko shrugged. "Lucky for me, the pass was so narrow they could only come at me one at a time. So I dealt with them one at a time, concentrating on the task in front of me. Somehow I was able to hold in there long enough that the Baskan commander called a halt to reclaim their dead and try to reason with me. He offered me the chance to settle it by a duel then, which I accepted."

Belasko took his plate and moved out of the line, taking another slice of melon. He continued to talk to Ervan, but by now all the other students, and Markus himself, were openly listening.

"I fought the duel with the Baskan champion and won. Much to my surprise."

"How did you win?" asked Markus, speaking from the back of the group that had by now gathered around Belasko as he told his tale. "You must have been beyond tired."

Belasko swallowed. "I didn't have a choice. It was kill or be killed, and after surviving that day, I had no intention of dying if I could possibly avoid it. I *was* exhausted though, so I barely even raised my blade to begin with. I focused on getting out of the way, waiting for my time to strike." He took another bite of melon, chewed and swallowed. "Which was when I got their champion turned around to face the setting sun. It blinded him."

Markus laughed, but judging from Ervan's expression, the story appalled him. "But-but that's dishonourable!" the courtier spluttered.

Belasko shrugged. "There's precious little honour in war, I'm afraid to say, and it was him or me. There's a little more to it than that, but I've no desire to relive that fight blow for blow."

Markus spoke up. "Our friend has just given you all a valuable lesson. In a duel, you have two options: kill or be killed. Everything else is unimportant, just dressing up those two things." The class turned now to face him. "Be assured, when you face someone in a duel, what matters most is your intention. It is not a fencing lesson or a bout to be scored. It is a battle. A desperate battle to the death. If you treat it as anything other than that, you will almost certainly lose. Especially if the other duellist has any idea what they're about. Remember this. It is in some ways what matters above all else, even skill. The swordsman's intent. Kill or be killed." He clapped his hands. "Finish up your food. Belasko has given us all something to think about, but we must move on. Back into your pairs."

Belasko winked at Ervan. "Come on. Let's get through this afternoon. I'll tell you the full story over a drink some time."

As they moved to take up their places once more, Ervan

could only shake his head. *Who is this rough, uncultured man? He's not what I expected a hero to be.*

That night, after an interminable day's training, Ervan went home disheartened. As he walked through the front door of his family townhouse, his mother appeared. Ervan barely noticed the footman who appeared, as if from nowhere, to take his cloak and boots, slipping into the slippers he provided with the easy familiarity of long practice.

"So, how did it go?" Lavinia asked. She sniffed when he only grunted in response. "Come into the back parlour. I've had cook put together a light supper for you. I want to hear all about it."

Ervan followed her through into the parlour, where he piled his plate before retreating to a comfortable chair to pick at the delicacies.

"To judge from your expression, today did not go as intended. What happened?" Lavinia frowned at him. Today she was dressed in a white, cream, and pale blue ensemble, with pearl buttons and delicate lacework by the yard. "You're one of the best swordsmen in the city. How can it have gone badly?"

"Belasko," Ervan muttered around a mouthful of pastry. "A common soldier. Dear god, he's fast. His technique is rough, but I've faced no one like him before. We were training together today, running through basic exercises, and I could barely get a touch on him."

"Belasko?" Lavinia's delicately plucked eyebrows climbed high on her forehead. "The hero of Dellan Pass? That Belasko?"

Ervan sighed. "That's the one. Magnificent warrior of the

Baskan War, come to show us a thing or two. I'd hate him if he wasn't so likeable."

"That's no reason not to hate him, son. If he takes this opportunity away from you, then our whole family will be set against him. You need this position at court. As our third child, you won't inherit much, if any, of this." Lavinia waved her hand in the air in a vague attempt to indicate all their wealth and the trappings thereof. "You need to make your own path. Beat this man and all the others. Be the best."

"Don't you think I'm trying?" Ervan snapped at his mother. "He's not normal. He's too damn quick. How can I beat him? It's all I can do to equal him."

Lavinia stepped forward, taking her son's face in both hands. "Listen here. So what if he's quicker? You're better. You've had access to all the best fencing masters, dedicated yourself to the art of swordplay. Your technique, the skills and tricks you've built up—they are better than him. Find a way."

Ervan sighed. "Yes, Mother."

As Belasko didn't reside in the city, he was offered accommodation in the old barracks building where they were training. The barracks had been built to house a large contingent of the City Watch, and as there weren't that many students, those who were resident were each given one of the rooms intended for officers. This guaranteed a certain amount of privacy and was more pleasant than sharing one of the dormitories normally reserved for the lower ranks.

It was a mixed group that sat down to the dinner provided that night—a rich stew with chunky bread served alongside watered wine. Conversation was scarce as those gathered sated their appetites. Some headed back for seconds and thirds. It had been a long and tiring day.

Eventually, replete, Belasko pushed back his plate and settled into his chair with a sigh. "Now that was a damn sight better than the provisions I've been getting of late."

Byrta, a cavalry officer, chewed and swallowed her mouthful before replying. "Have you been out on manoeuvres? Our food's normally good at the barracks."

"Ours too." Belasko nodded. "Yes, we've been out marching around the countryside and working through training exercises. The war might be over, but we need to show we're still active, still sharp, in case the Baskans get any more ideas. And we've got to blood in these recent recruits we've picked up in peacetime somehow."

"I was due out with my squadron in the next few days, for the same reasons. Instead, here I am." Byrta shrugged. "I'm honoured to have been invited, but there's not much chance any of us will become the Champion. The role will probably go to one of the posh lot."

"I don't know about that," said Umbert, a large and well-muscled man who was surprisingly quick for his size. "Markus doesn't come from wealth—not one of the founding families at least, is what I heard. I don't think he'll favour them all that much."

"You've got a chance, surely, Belasko? The glorious hero, the man who stood alone against the Baskan army. Sounds like Champion material to me!" This last, accompanied by a sarcastic eye-roll, came from Artur, a hawk-faced man whose tone was as sharp as his appearance.

Belasko's smile was a little forced. "It wasn't quite like that." His smile faded. "I don't know who of us has a chance. I'll tell you what though, the man they partnered me with today, Ervan. He was good. Very good. It's been a long time since I've faced anyone that good with a blade, if ever."

There was silence at this, which eventually Byrta broke with a cough. "Was he that skilled?"

Belasko nodded. "It's been a long time since I've struggled so much against an opponent."

"Aye, but you're better. I'm sure you landed more touches than him. I was watching," said Umbert.

"Is that why you were so rubbish during our exercise? Your attention was elsewhere?" A slight smile took the sting out of Artur's words, but Umbert still flushed.

"All right lads, that's enough. You can bet the posh lot will work together. We'd best do the same. No fighting amongst ourselves." Byrta's countenance was stern.

"What about what Markus said?" Belasko asked. "About us all being students together? Who we are outside these walls doesn't matter, or isn't supposed to."

Artur snorted. "Idealistic nonsense. Markus has been too long at court, forgotten what it's like to be a nobody in the eyes of the high and mighty. They respect him because of who he is, his position at court, his proximity to the king. We don't have that advantage. He's earned their respect."

"So has Belasko, if you think about it." Umbert waved a hand in his direction. "He's a hero. Everyone knows about his actions in the war."

Artur gave a cynical laugh, shaking his head. "Crawl out of his arse Umbert, Belasko's good with a blade. That's all. Doesn't mean we should worship him."

Belasko coughed, somewhat uncomfortable. "I don't know how much leverage my past gives me, but I'm of a mind to take Markus at his word. Give things a go his way." He shrugged. "You're all my comrades in arms. In battle, I'd give my life for any of you. Here we are students again,

Markus's, and I say we do things the way he wants." The soldier grinned. "At least until the little lords and ladies show they're not playing along." The rest of them laughed. Belasko's face straightened, serious again. "Now, help me figure out how to improve against this Ervan fellow. I want to beat him tomorrow."

**2**

Ervan stepped back and wiped the sweat from his brow as Markus called a break. If anything, Belasko was even faster today, and he had yet to land a touch on the soldier. Ervan, meanwhile, had deployed every trick at his disposal and had kept Belasko at bay. The war hero was also yet to land a touch on him.

He nodded to Belasko as they made their way into the line for refreshments. "You seem faster today than yesterday. Did you fit in some extra practice last night?"

Belasko shook his head. "No, yesterday I was tired from my journey. Last night I slept well and woke feeling refreshed." He grinned. "Although I will admit to having a brief discussion over dinner last night with the others staying here. It was useful to pick the day apart with them." His grin widened. "And for getting a few tips on moves to use against you."

"So would you say that staying here gives you an advantage in your training?"

Belasko mused this over for a moment as they moved

forward in the line. "I suppose it does. It helps to talk things over with the other students."

Ervan reached the front of the line, pouring himself a glass of sweet fruit juice. "I may ask Markus if I can stay here, while we're training."

The grin shrank a little. "I'm sure you'd be welcome."

"Good. Well then, no time like the present." Ervan peeled off from the group and walked over to Markus, who was in conversation with Byrta. Their conversation finished as Ervan approached. Byrta nodded at what Markus had to say and left to join the queue for refreshments.

Markus looked up as the student approached. "Ervan, how are you finding things? I've been observing you and Belasko closely. You've both impressed me."

"Thank you. I think things are going rather well. I have to admit that it's nice to be pushed. I don't think I've had to work this hard against an opponent... well, ever."

Markus smiled. "Yes, Belasko is something special, is he not? As are you. As is everyone here. Choosing my successor will be no straightforward task! Anyway, what can I do for you?"

"I was talking with Belasko, and he said he found it helpful staying here with some of the other students. They could discuss the day's training over dinner and offer each other ideas and suggestions. I was wondering if it would be possible to stay here as well, while we're training."

Markus nodded. "Yes, of course. All are welcome. I just assumed those with homes in the city would prefer to stay in more comfortable, familiar surroundings. In fact..." He cleared his throat, then called out. "Everyone, gather around me when you've got such food and drink as you desire."

They passed a few moments discussing the day's training, Markus offering Ervan some feedback and tips, while the others gathered. When all were ready and listening, Markus spoke.

"It has come to my attention that those staying here, in this old barracks, have found it helpful staying together. That last night, over dinner, they could pick apart the day's training and offer each other help and support. It strikes me that this is a good thing. So I would like to make a clear invitation to all of you to stay here, if you would like to."

Which was how all the students came to stay at the barracks.

"Thanks for this, Belasko. I'm so glad the little lords and ladies have joined our group. It's so cosy," Byrta said under her breath.

Belasko flushed. "Yes, well, I didn't know Ervan would want to room with us. Let alone that the rest would follow suit." He looked down the length of the table at those gathered for dinner. Their group now comprised all twenty of Markus's students, and they had arranged themselves around the table by social order without thinking: the children of nobility and wealthy families at one end, the commoners and soldiers at the other. The conversation was a little more muted than it had been the previous evening.

Anerin, one of the nobility, cleared his throat before addressing the table. "Now that supper's over, I've arranged for some decent brandy for all of us. To help, um, ease the conversation somewhat." A stocky young man with dun coloured hair, his features seemed too coarse to sit well among the courtly finery he wore. He clapped his hands, and a server appeared with a small barrel that they set on a side table and, with a speed and precision that spoke of long practice, tapped. Several others followed them in carrying decanters which were filled quickly and placed around the table, a brandy glass appearing at every diner's side.

"Very kind of you," said Umbert, holding his glass up in salute. "Very kind."

Anerin waved away the compliment. "Not at all. We are all, after all, brothers and sisters in arms under Markus's ministrations. We should relax, get to know each other. Also, Belasko, if I remember correctly, you said you'd tell Ervan the story of Dellan Pass over a drink some time... the full story. I'm sure you wouldn't mind if we listened in."

Belasko made a face. "Another time, perhaps. There are others here who served in the war. They no doubt have their own stories to tell. Personally, I'd like to hear those, if they're willing to share? But first, a toast." He raised the glass which a server had filled and handed to him. "To comrades in arms —those we've fought beside, those we've lost, and those who survived. And to new friends."

"Comrades in arms," chorused the rest of the group before each taking a swallow of their brandy.

Belasko made an appreciative face. "Now that is better than I'm used to. What we drink in the field tastes like it's been brewed in someone's boots." There was laughter at this. "Now, I'm already sick of the sound of my own voice. Who has a story to tell?"

Artur grinned. "It's not what you'd call heroic, but I do have an enjoyable story about a senior officer caught in a compromising situation with a goat. If there's any interest in that sort of thing."

There was distaste on the faces of some present, but Anerin laughed. "Well," he said, "not all war stories have to be noble. I'm happy to trade a tale or two, but I don't think my own anecdotes of fencing matches and courtly dances quite live up to your war stories. Particularly not that one. Although I think being descended on by a number of eligible ladies at one of the palace balls might be only mildly less terrifying than facing down a horde of Baskans."

"Were they terribly savage? The Baskans you all fought?" asked Bryn, a slender young man with dark hair and a swarthy complexion, the top fencing student from the provincial city of Ellam. He had so far more than held his own against the best the capital could offer.

Byrta gestured with her brandy glass, taking in the group. "I can't speak for any of the others here who served in the war, but I found them no more or less savage than any professional fighter. They were there to do a job, which was to kill or defeat us, and we had our own duties likewise." She took a sip of her brandy. "Most of the time, war is mind-numbingly dull. A lot of marching, or riding, or standing guard and hoping not to get caught napping by your senior officer. Or an enemy combatant, for that matter. Then, for a small period, it's utter mind-bending terror and a desperate struggle to stay alive." She shrugged. "Mostly, the soldiers in any war have more in common with each other than they have differences. I'll tell you this though: they are a martial race, which some might confuse with savagery. They base their society around the military. Every court functionary, every ambassador, has a military rank alongside their civilian duties. But while they're warlike in their aspect, they have honour."

Belasko nodded. "I'd agree with that. Take General Edyard, who I met at Dellan Pass. He acted honourably. In fact, when I exited the pass to go to the Baskan camp, their entire force was massed in ranks before me. On a whim, I saluted them—those whose comrades had fought and died so bravely in trying to take the pass. They returned the salute, the whole damn lot of them. We might have been enemies on the battlefield, but that day we were brothers and sisters in war."

He paused, aware that the room had gone silent. Belasko looked up to see a variety of expressions on the faces that regarded him. There was understanding on the faces of his fellow soldiers, confusion and puzzlement on the others. He sighed. "This is why I don't enjoy telling stories. The world is a more complicated place than the bards sing of. It doesn't fit so easily into a jovial tale." He held up his glass. "I think I need more brandy now."

As the following day was due to be a rest day, when Anerin suggested they continue their evening's drinking at a tavern he knew, close to the barracks, everyone decided it was an excellent idea. So they piled out into the street, Anerin leading the way. Spirits were high, and they chatted and laughed as they left the barracks. Movement across the street caught Belasko's eye. A figure who had been leaning against a wall opposite the barracks' entrance turned and ducked into an alleyway. It was only a fraction of a second, but Belasko caught an impression of olive skin and long dark hair.

Byrta noticed him pause. She peered in the direction he was looking. "What is it? Everything all right?"

Belasko frowned. "I'm sure it's nothing, but... I think someone was watching the barracks. They were leaning against that wall but left as we came out."

Byrta laughed. "What, is there a law against leaning on walls now? I'm sure someone was just taking their ease before carrying on their way. Nothing to worry about. Now come on, we've got some drinking to do." They both quickened their step to catch up with the others, who were now some way down the street, and hastened off on their night of revelry.

To the surprise of Belasko and his fellow soldiers, the courtiers and more genteel among them could hold their drink just as well as they. By the time they had journeyed to the fifth tavern on their little expedition, it was perhaps no longer such an excellent idea.

They had lost a few of their fellow revellers along the way—those who decided they'd had enough, or that in this instance discretion was the better part of valour. As they moved from drinking establishment to drinking establishment, the areas in which they found themselves became progressively more disreputable. They took a large table in the final tavern, attracting a lot of interested looks from the rougher types at the bar. Any untoward attention was dissuaded by the swords at their hips and the fact that, even in an advanced state of inebriation, they moved like they knew how to use them.

"Why have we ended up here?" Belasko asked Anerin, who slouched on a bench next to him, peering into his tankard as if it contained the answers to the mysteries of the universe. "We started off in much better places."

Anerin raised his eyes, blinking owlishly at Belasko. "Don't wanna be too drunk in the nice places, y'see. As our condition gets worse, so should our surroundings. Don't wanna make a scene where it'll be seen. Do y'see?"

Belasko nodded. In their current condition, this sounded like wise advice indeed. He shifted in his seat, aware of a pressing need that had arisen. "Do you know this place well?" Anerin nodded. "Good. Any idea where I might find the privy?"

"Out back." Anerin waved vaguely at the rear entrance. "Other side of the alleyway."

Belasko got to his feet, stumbling slightly, and made his way in the direction the young lord had indicated. At the back of the room, he found a wooden door that led onto a narrow and poorly lit alley, the privies opposite the doorway. He crossed to them, opened the door, and ventured in, blinking a little at the odour.

After he had finished attending to the necessary, he exited the privies to find five figures in the alleyway, waiting. They wore dark clothing, cloaked and hooded, and in the poor light, it wasn't possible to make out their faces.

"Sorry, I hope you weren't waiting too long. Watch out for the smell. That wasn't me, by the way. Well, not all me." The figures parted to let Belasko through. As he passed by, he heard a whisper of cloth and saw something gleam in the moonlight—something in the hand of the figure to his right. He let out a shout, leaping forward and twisting to the side, moving around them as he drew his sword. Belasko raised it just in time to deflect a blow from what was now more clearly a short sword, the other four drawing their own weapons.

Although he was the worse for drink, his reactions and movements slower and less coordinated than usual, Belasko still planned to put up a fight. He gave another yell and leaped forward, his blade thrusting towards the figure who had first attacked him, before diverting the blow to ward off an attack from another quarter. His sword wove a web of steel before him, glinting in the light of the moon, as he took on all five attackers at once.

His opponents were clearly not used to fighting together, and the cramped confines of the alleyway meant that they got in each other's way. For the moment, Belasko was able to hold his own against them. The rush of energy and fear that ran through him burned away many of the ill effects of the alcohol. Still, he knew five against one weren't odds that normally went in the single combatant's favour.

Umbert and Ervan appeared at the back door of the inn, both swaying slightly. "Is there a bit of a queue?" The bigger man asked. He peered at the events unfolding before him. "Oh, bugger. Belasko, is that you?"

Ervan looked from Umbert to the desperate fight taking place in front of them and sighed. He drew his own sword, and said, "Ah well, we'd best give you a hand then," before falling on Belasko's attackers from the rear. Umbert drew his sword and, roaring a challenge, threw himself into the fray.

The next minute was a blur, as Umbert, Belasko and Ervan fought furiously for their lives. The assailants, fighting now on two fronts against highly skilled opponents, gave ground. Inch by inch, they backed towards the entrance to the alley. "Now!" shouted one of the hooded figures, and they leaped to the attack with renewed energy and speed. As they sprung forwards, one of their hoods slipped back, revealing a woman with long black hair and the olive complexion of a Baskan. She gritted her teeth, frustrated at having revealed herself, but couldn't spare a moment to pull up her hood.

*That's who I saw opposite the barracks, I'm sure of it.* The thought came unbidden to Belasko's mind as, for a few frantic seconds, he and his comrades were hard-pressed to defend themselves. However, faced with something other than the easy kill they had expected, the cloaked figures turned as one and ran from the alley. Umberto, moving with a speed surprising in one his size, threw himself forwards and grabbed one assailant by their cloak. He yanked them back towards him, and they tumbled to the ground together in a jumble of limbs and sharp steel. Belasko moved to follow the others on instinct but pulled up short hearing a cry from Umbert.

"Belasko!" He turned to find Umbert sitting on the ground next to the cloaked figure he had apprehended, sword abandoned beside him, clutching his right thigh as blood welled between his fingers. The big man's face was pale. "Bastard stuck me at the end there. Just got through my guard, but they came off worse." He nodded at the lifeless figure next to him, blood pooling around them. Ervan inspected the cloaked figure cautiously, prodding them with the toe of his boot. The movement rolled them onto their back, and lifeless eyes gazed up at the narrow patch of night sky above the alley. Ervan gulped, his face turning pale.

Belasko took this in as he sheathed his own sword and dropped down beside Umbert, inspecting the wound. "The blood isn't pumping out, so I don't think they've hit anything critical, but we need to clean that and get you to someone who can patch you up properly. Wait here. I'll get the others. Ervan, keep him company."

Belasko ran back into the tavern, finding their group's table quickly. The look on his face stopped any ongoing frivolity in its tracks. "I was attacked in the alley. Umbert and Ervan came to my aid. We fought them off, killed one of them, but Umbert's taken an injury to his leg. Can someone who knows the city better than me find a doctor and bring them here quickly?"

Anerin stood, downing the rest of his drink. "There's a pretty reputable doctor in this quarter, I know where. If I go now, I can be back in just a few minutes."

"Go then, and fast. Somebody else help us bring him inside. We need to get him seen to and back to the barracks as soon as we can. We'd best send for the city watch as well and organise someone to stay with the body."

~

As Byrta oversaw the group carrying Umbert into the tavern, Ervan and Belasko looked down at the dead body of their attacker.

"You've summoned the watch, I take it?," said Ervan.

Belasko nodded. "Already taken care of. The landlord has sent a runner. They'll be here soon. Someone will have to stay behind to talk to them and oversee things here."

"I'll do it. They'll have some questions for you, I'm sure, but we can get that over with quickly so you can get Umbert back to the barracks. They can follow up in more detail tomorrow."

Belasko smiled at the young courtier. "You seem sure of yourself."

Ervan laughed. "Listen, daring charges and fights against the odds might be among your skills, but this is my area of expertise. I know the way this city works and, trust me, we can use our positions to make things go the way we want them."

"Positions?" Belasko frowned, not understanding.

Ervan pointed at Belasko. "Glorious war hero." Then he pointed at himself. "Son of a noble house, one of the oldest in Villan. Trust me. Let me talk to the watch when they arrive."

"All right, I will. And Ervan, thank you. For coming to my aid tonight." Belasko held out his hand, which Ervan took to shake. Then corrected himself, shifting to the warriors' grip, wrist to wrist.

He smiled at Belasko. "Not at all. Now, one day, I can tell my children that I fought alongside the hero of Dellan Pass."

The city watch came and, as Ervan predicted, asked a few questions to establish what had happened before taking custody of the body. They made note of who was involved in the attack, where they were staying, and promised to pay them a visit the next day with any follow-up questions.

At the same time, as Anerin returned with the local doctor, they checked Umbert over. His injury cleaned and bandaged, Belasko and some of the others hired a carriage to get their injured friend back to the old barracks. The rest, their mood for revelry by now quite dampened, made their own way back by slower and sometimes more circuitous routes.

Despite the lateness of the hour, Markus was waiting for them at the old barracks' gates when they returned. Somehow he already knew some of what had befallen them.

"How bad is it?" he asked, opening the carriage door almost before it had halted, concern writ large across his face.

"It's but a scratch," said Umbert, smiling weakly. "I've had worse."

Markus took in his pale demeanour and frowned. "Yes. Well, I'll be happier once my own physician has looked you over. Luckily this place still has a serviceable infirmary, and she's on call, in case of any incidents during training. Come on," he said, reaching up a hand to help Umbert down. "Let's get you inside."

With the help of Belasko, Byrta, and Artur, he got the larger man out of the carriage and into the barracks.

They ensured Umbert was settled into a bed in the infirmary, a long low building with two rows of beds but only one occupant. Markus's physician, Maelyn, was a small wiry woman, her black hair shot through with silver, and a pair of wire-framed spectacles perched on the end of her nose. She looked Umbert over, while Markus turned to Umbert's companions.

"Thank you all for helping your brother in arms tonight and bringing him swiftly home. I think you should all find your beds and secure your own rest. Belasko, if I could speak with you for a moment?"

The others, dismissed, all filed out, calling their good-byes to Umbert as they left. He smiled and waved, then winced as Maelyn probed his wound.

Markus drew Belasko to one side, speaking in hushed tones. "What happened tonight? The information that reached me was garbled, but I know you were at the centre of it."

Belasko sighed. "It doesn't make much sense to me. We all went out for a drink, all the students together. The last place we ended up was a little, um, disreputable, but we had no trouble inside. I used the privy, which was outside the main tavern building and across a little alley. When I emerged, five people attacked me—cloaked and hooded, all carrying short swords. Umbert and Ervan came outside, saw what was happening, and leaped to my aid. Together we fought them off. In the last moments of the fight, Umbert took the injury to his thigh while bringing down and killing an attacker."

Markus frowned. "Did these people make any attempt to rob you, or introduce themselves in any way?"

Belasko shook his head. "No, they said nothing. Just drew their swords and attacked."

"You say Umbert killed one of them. What happened to the body?"

"We called for the city watch, who came and took it. They asked a few questions but said they would visit tomorrow to follow up."

Markus nodded. "And what became of the others? Was there anything to identify them?"

"No." Belasko hung his head. "Actually... there is one thing." He looked up, meeting Markus's gaze. "When we left tonight, I saw some movement across from the barracks entrance. Someone leaning against the wall, who ducked into the alleyway. It was only a brief moment, but I saw them. Long black hair and olive skin. During the fight, one of the attackers' hoods slipped, and we could see their face. It was a woman with the same colouring. She looked Baskan, to be honest."

Markus looked into the middle distance, lips pursed in thought. "This wasn't an attempted robbery. You were their target." He met Belasko's gaze, eyes fierce. "One of you will be my successor, and that makes all of you valuable. But I will make it known that you are all under my personal protection. Anyone who attempts to harm my students goes against me, and therefore against the king. That should calm down whoever set this up. A Baskan presence adds another complication though. I'll speak to the city watch myself when they come tomorrow, see if I can find out what they think is going on. I can talk to their commander."

"Is this what it's like? Being the King's Champion?"

Markus nodded. "It's part of it. Bear that in mind, Belasko, should you be the one to follow in my footsteps: that you are walking into a web of palace intrigue." He looked over as Maelyn gestured for his attention. "Say your goodnights to Umbert. I need to talk with Maelyn for a moment." He walked off a ways with the physician, talking in the same hushed tone he had used with Belasko.

Belasko walked over to Umbert's bedside and clasped the big man's hand. "How are you feeling?"

Umbert shrugged. "Not too bad. As I said outside, I've had worse. Still, that's me out of the running to replace Markus now. According to the doctor, this should heal well, but it will take time. No leaping about for a while."

"I'm sorry. It's not fair. You were injured trying to help me..."

"I'd do it again in a heartbeat." Umbert smiled. "The doctor told me I should get some rest. You could use some beauty sleep yourself."

"All right, but I'll come by to see you in the morning. Good night, Umbert."

"Good night, Belasko."

Belasko turned and left the infirmary alone with his thoughts and sought his bed.

The next morning, Ervan visited his mother at their family home in the city. He was welcomed in by a footman and quickly ushered into her favourite parlour. Lavinia was there, delicately sipping from a cup of tea as she read a book of Navitian verse. She set both aside to welcome her son, taking him by the shoulders and kissing him upon the cheek before gesturing to a chair across from her own.

"Welcome home, son. Please, sit, and tell me how your training goes."

He took up her invitation, settling into the comfortable chair with a sigh. He gave her a sly smile. "You act as if I've been gone for weeks, not just a few days. You can't be missing me around the house that much?"

Lavinia sniffed. "Of course not. Can't a mother be happy to see her youngest son? I'm excited to hear your news, that's all."

"It's much of a muchness. The training continues well. I have the measure of the other students, except Belasko. I'll spare you the details. There was a bit of excitement last night, however."

Lavinia arched a delicately pencilled brow. "Oh? Do tell."

"As today is a rest day anyway, all the students went out for a drink together yesterday evening. At Anerin's prompting."

"Why am I not surprised? Too fond of the drink, that boy." Lavinia shook her head.

"Yes, well, be that as it may, he suggested an evening of rabble-rousing intoxication and we gladly followed his suggestion. All was going well—it was quite an enjoyable evening, actually—until we reached the final venue for the evening's entertainments. A disreputable tavern in the outer quarters, you'll no doubt be scandalised to hear, where towards the end of the evening Belasko, having gone outside to use the necessary, was set upon by five assailants. We think at least one of them was Baskan..." His mother's expectant expression caused him to trail off. "But you already know all about it, don't you? Mother, how do you know? What have you done?"

"Only what *needed* to be done." She took a sip of her tea. "Do you remember your great aunt, Alvia? Married to a Baskan gentleman a long time before all the recent unpleasantness between our peoples. I wrote to her, informing her of how you were competing to take Markus's place as Royal

Champion. The great honour it would bring to our house if you were to do so, and that a common soldier, one Belasko, stood in your way. Of course, I told her to keep this information in strictest confidence, sure there are factions in Baskan society that wish harm on Belasko for his actions in the Last War... However, it sounds like the information may have got into the wrong hands." She put her cup and saucer down on the table next to her chair before folding her hands in her lap. "Did you think for one moment I would sit idly by and let some commoner take this position from you?"

"I can't believe you. No, actually, I can. I'm just disappointed. First, the attackers failed. Belasko held them off long enough for one of the other students and I to come to his aid. Umbert—who isn't talented enough to have been a threat to me—was injured, but Belasko escaped unscathed."

Lavinia's face took on a disappointed cast. "Oh."

"'Oh' indeed. Second, I'm upset. I was just starting to get along with the others. I even thought there might be the possibility of building some friendships there. How can I be friends with them now, when I know this attack was all your fault?" Ervan stood and paced the room, gesticulating wildly as anger took over. "Third, I'm insulted. Insulted that you thought I needed help of this sort to win my place as Markus's successor. I can do this on my own, Mother, on my own merits and skill. This behaviour..." He turned to face her. "If I don't win this fairly, I don't win it at all. I wouldn't deserve it."

He moved closer, kneeling by her chair. "Mother, I can do this. I will do this, without foul play."

Lavinia sighed. "Oh Ervan, how could you be friends with those others? You're a member of one of the oldest noble families in Villan. We can trace our lineage right back to the founding of the city. They're peasants, some of them, so far beneath you. I..." She shook her head. "I thought I raised you to be above such foolish concepts as honour. That you wouldn't be one of these fools who spends their time tripping over their own dignity rather than getting things done." She gave him a piercing look. "What matters is who wins, not how they play the game." She sniffed again. "However, if that is what you want, then so be it. You will win your place on your own merits. Or not."

**3**

That same morning, as Ervan was visiting his mother, Belasko returned to the infirmary after breakfast and brought with him Byrta and Artur. The infirmary's sole occupant was himself in the last stages of demolishing what had been a substantial tray of food. He looked up as they entered and waved them over. Mouth full, he grinned as they approached.

"Doctor said I need to eat up, rebuild my strength."

"I'm not sure your strength is in question. Or your appetite," said Artur, a sly expression on his face.

"Hush Artur, our comrade here was wounded while bravely protecting a friend." Byrta patted Umbert on the shoulder. "He can have all the breakfast he wants."

"Well then, I might send down for seconds." He laughed at the look on their faces. "Only joking, I've had my fill."

"How are you feeling?" Belasko asked, a concerned expression on his face.

Umbert shrugged. "All right, I suppose. The doctor took another look at me this morning and is just as convinced that the wound will heal well. If anything, the greater injury is knowing I'll miss out on the rest of the training. This journey is over for me."

Belasko sighed. "I'm so sorry, Umbert. It's all my fault. You were injured coming to help me. I—"

"Stop that, Belasko. Blame the people that attacked you and gave me this." The large man gestured to where his leg lay, covered by blankets. "It's their fault, not yours." His genial face took on a grim expression. "But don't doubt that you were the target, Belasko. You're the best of us, and I'd wager gold that someone doesn't want a commoner as King's Champion."

"No. I think they may have been Baskan agents. I mean, why would someone...?" Belasko faltered.

"Come on Belasko, it's the only thing that makes sense. I don't see a horde of Baskans in the city, clamouring for revenge for Dellan Pass." He looked at each of them in turn. "Promise me this: you won't let them win. All of you, you'll work hard, work together, to ensure the title of Champion doesn't go to one of these spoiled little lordlings."

"But why? Why does background matter?" asked Belasko.

Artur scoffed. "A commoner with the ear of the king? That's too good an opportunity to pass up. Think of the good they could do, the changes they might bring." He reached over to clasp Umbert's hand. "I promise I'll do all I can to ensure one of us wins the right to succeed Markus." He let Umbert's hand drop and glared at the other two. "What about you?"

Byrta copied him, taking Umbert's hand. "I promise. One of us will succeed. I'll give it everything I have."

Belasko looked at them, meeting their gazes one by one, then nodded. "All right, I promise. We'll do everything we can to win this competition and make sure the role of

Champion goes to someone with an ounce of common sense. We'll work together, help each other, hold extra training when the others are resting. Whatever it takes."

"Good." Umbert nodded, satisfied. Then he looked down at his empty breakfast tray. "I've changed my mind. I will have seconds. Could you send down to the kitchen for another tray?"

As Belasko and the others left the infirmary and Umbert to enjoy his second breakfast, Markus was waiting outside.

"Good morning all, sorry to interrupt. Belasko, if I might borrow you for a moment? The city watch are here and have some further questions about last night."

Belasko nodded. "Of course." He turned to the others. "I'll catch up with you later."

"All right," said Byrta, "try not to incriminate yourself."

The others continued on their way down the corridor as Belasko went with Markus in the other direction.

"Where are we going?" he asked the Royal Champion.

"My study. The watch Commander is waiting there."

That brought Belasko up short. "The watch Commander? Am I in trouble?"

Markus laughed. "No, not at all. She has a few questions about last night and some news about your attackers. She just wanted to talk to you in person."

Belasko walked on with the older man in silence, wondering what the news might be. They made their way to Markus's study fairly quickly. The door was open, and the watch Commander sat inside waiting for them.

The room that Markus had taken for himself served as his office and study. It wasn't large, and the writing desk against the wall had seen better days, as had the mismatched chairs set around it. The chair opposite the one Markus must normally sit in was occupied by Alliarin, Commander of the Villanese city watch. She stood when they entered, a former military officer who Belasko knew by reputation if not by sight. She was a well-muscled woman with short-cropped steel grey hair, clad in a more refined version of the brown and grey uniform that was the hallmark of the city watch. A golden badge of rank adorned her breastplate, her armour solid and well made.

Alliarin looked to Markus, raising her eyebrows. "Is this him?" Markus nodded, taking his seat behind the desk. "Very well." She turned her gaze on Belasko. "I have some questions for you, and some information. First, I've had the report given by the officers that attended the incident last night, but I'd like to hear it again from your own lips. So, please, tell me everything you remember." She sat again but did not indicate that he should do the same.

Belasko shifted into the "at ease" position that he assumed when reporting to superior officers, years of habit and training coming to the fore. He told her everything that had happened the previous evening, as well as he could recall.

Alliarin sat for a moment after he had finished, drumming her fingers on the arm of her chair while she looked into space. She turned her gaze back to Belasko. "This person you saw outside the barracks: how sure are you it was the same woman whose face you saw during the attack?"

Belasko shrugged. "As certain as I can be. I only caught the briefest glimpse of them as we left, but the colouring and hair matched. I think it would be too much of a coincidence otherwise."

"And you're positive that they were Baskan?"

"Yes. I came face to face with enough of their people during the war to be sure of that."

"Very well, that chimes with some other information that has come to light." Alliarin tilted her head to one side, regarding Belasko for a long moment before speaking again. "The attacker that your friend killed, we are certain they were a Baskan agent. I can't go into too much detail, but certain items they were carrying confirmed that for us." She shook her head. "They must really hate you, boy. It's safe to assume that you were the focus of the attack. I would suggest that you be on your guard, but I have a feeling you always are. War does that to a person. In the meantime, don't leave this building on your own. If you have to go outside, be careful. No hanging out by privies in dead-end alleyways, for example. We'll add some extra patrols to the surrounding streets, but my feeling is that having failed in this attack, they'll think twice about acting again soon." Alliarin stood. "Now, if you'll excuse me, gentlemen, I have other things to attend to today. I'd ask you to keep this information to yourselves. It wouldn't do to have the general population aware that Baskan agents are at large in the city."

As she made her way to the door, Belasko saluted her, instinctively. This raised a smile. "I like him," she said to Markus. "He has manners." Then to Belasko, "Don't get too used to throwing salutes. If you succeed Markus then you'd outrank me. Technically."

Alliarin went to leave but turned back into the room. She arched an eyebrow at Belasko. "You know, I thought you'd be taller." Then she left.

The following day, training was due to resume as normal, but without Umbert's participation. Ervan returned to the barracks early, just before dawn, and set to work. He intended to run through at least an hour of solo drills every morning before the other students entered the training area. Furious with his mother, he sought perfection in his movements, determined to win his place by right.

*I can't believe she did that*, he thought to himself as he wiped the sweat from his brow. *I can do this without her help. With no one's help.* He took a deep breath and settled himself into an attack stance, blade held high and ready to fall on anyone foolish enough to enter within its reach. *I can do this.*

Ervan worked for several hours, alone, before Markus arrived. The Royal Champion pushed open the door and paused, surprised to see anyone there before him. He let himself into the room, closing the door behind him, and observed Ervan for a moment. A slight smile played across his lips.

"Excellent form, Ervan. A distinct improvement. You're taking on board the lessons here."

Ervan, lost in his focus, was surprised by Markus's voice and stumbled slightly before righting himself and turning towards the older man. "Thank you, sir. I've been working through what you showed us in the previous session."

"I can see that. How long have you been here?" Markus stepped forward as he spoke, taking in Ervan's flushed complexion, the sweat beading on his forehead.

"An hour or so, sir. I've dedicated myself to this. I want to be the best."

Markus drew near to the young swordsman, smiling

again. "I admire your dedication. You remind me a little of myself when I was your age." He laughed. "Oh, how I wanted to beat them all. To prove myself. Remember though, Ervan, no man should seek to isolate himself. Your dedication does you credit, but don't just work alone. There is much you can learn from the other students here. That is why I brought you all together, to pool your experience and skills, see what emerges." Markus clapped Ervan on the shoulder. "Don't push yourself too hard. I will work you all today, and it will only get more difficult, more demanding. We're nearing the point where I will winnow out the weaker students. Nearing when, after that, I will make my decision. Don't exhaust yourself too early." The door opened, and a familiar figure entered. Markus looked up. "Ah, Belasko. Good morning. How are you today?"

Belasko smiled. "Well, thank you, sir."

"Good. Good." Markus clapped his hands. "As you're both here early, why don't you help me get things set up?"

"Of course," Belasko and Ervan chorused together. They looked at each other and laughed, then began to get out the equipment the students would need for the day.

As they worked, Belasko leaned over to Ervan. "Thank you for your help the other night. Without you and Umbert, well, I wouldn't be standing here now."

Ervan stiffened, an icy expression settling on his face. "Don't mention it. Any of us would have done the same."

Belasko shook his head. "Be that as it may, you were the one to come to my aid, so you're the one I'd like to thank."

"As I said, don't mention it. Really."

Ervan walked off, leaving Belasko with a puzzled expression on his face. He frowned. *I thought I'd finally got through that icy facade of his.* Then he shrugged, and it was forgotten. There was a day's training to be getting on with.

Later, after the day's training had finished, Belasko approached Markus with Byrta and Artur. Markus looked up from putting away his training blade in its polished hardwood case. He smiled at them as he flicked closed the clasps and then stood.

"Good work today, all three of you. What can I do for you?"

"Well, sir, we were wondering," said Byrta, "if it would be all right for us to stay behind for some extra training."

"Just us, sir," said Artur hurriedly. "We're not asking you to stay."

"And if we might let ourselves in after dinner, to work a little more?" asked Belasko.

Markus laughed. "Today is my day to see which students will put in a little extra effort, isn't it? This morning, when I arrived, I found that Ervan had been here for some time already. Running through solo drills." He sighed. "Of course you can undertake extra practice. I'm surprised no one has asked before now, in all honesty. What is it you hope to do?"

"Well, sir," said Belasko, "we all come from different branches of the military, have different training and skills. We thought we could learn something from each other. We can also practice drills against multiple opponents, run through exercises from the day's training, that sort of thing."

A wide smile spread across Markus's face. "Of course. Of course you can! This is what I hoped for when I brought all of you here—that you would work together, cooperate, learn from each other. Perfect. You can stay now and let yourselves in again later. Only don't exhaust yourselves. I'll tell you what I told Ervan this morning: our days together will only get harder." He bent and picked up his case from the floor. "Belasko, can I have a quick moment of your time?"

Markus drew Belasko away from the others as he moved towards the door. "Belasko, could you come to see me tonight, after dinner? Just pop by my study for a quick chat," he said quietly. Then he patted Belasko on the shoulder. "Nothing to worry about, but let's keep it between us. Now, if you'll excuse me, I'll leave you to your studies."

As Markus left the room, Belasko turned back to the others. He frowned, ignoring the quizzical look on their faces. "Did anyone else find that last drill from today tricky? Shall we run through that again first?"

Artur nodded. Byrta said, "Yes, and that riposte that Markus showed us this morning. I couldn't quite get the angle with my wrist."

"Good, that's somewhere to start." Belasko nodded to them both. "Let's begin."

Belasko came to a halt at the entrance to the corridor leading to Markus's study. He was brought up short both by surprise and the actual impediment of two guards barring his way. They wore plain attire, with no sigils or tabards to show which house or family they served, but their armour was well made and of impressive quality. Whoever they served, their wealth wasn't in question.

The guard to the left, a tall man with dull red coloured hair, spoke first. "Hold. What is your business here?"

"Markus asked that I attend him this evening. He wanted to talk to me about something. What are you doing here? There aren't normally guards posted to Markus's quarters." Belasko peered over their shoulders, curious more than nervous. He could see a further two guards stationed outside the door to Markus's study, and yet two more at the other end of the corridor where it led on to another hallway.

"Oi, what are you looking at?" asked the guard to the right, a broad-shouldered woman with a fierce countenance. "We'll ask the questions, thank you very much."

"Just wondering who has come calling. I can come back later, but this is the time Markus asked me to come. Perhaps he wanted me to meet his guest?" Belasko shrugged. "As I said, I can come back later. If you'll just let Markus know that I've come by so he doesn't think I ignored his request."

The two guards exchanged a look. "All right," said the fierce-looking woman. "Ogrin here will let him know you've called, and we'll see if he wants you to meet our master."

The red-haired man, now identified as Ogrin, nodded. "It's not beyond the realm of possibility, Arjana. Who can I say has come calling?"

"Belasko."

The two guards blinked, surprised at this information.

"Belasko, as in..." Ogrin looked at Arjana.

"Yes, Dellan Pass. That Belasko."

Ogrin nodded, giving an appreciative whistle. "Well, I'll be. It might be our master would like to meet you after all. Hang on here a moment. Don't give Arjana any trouble while I'm gone." With that, he turned and walked down the corridor.

Arjana held out her hand, which Belasko took and shook. "It's a pleasure to meet you, Belasko. You're one of the big heroes from the Last War. The stories of your exploits, well..." She shook her head. "Let's just say they've made an impression on a lot of us in the guard." She tilted her head to one side, an appraising look in her eyes.

"Don't take this the wrong way, but I thought you'd be taller."

Belasko grinned at her. "I get that a lot."

Down the corridor, Ogrin knocked on the study door. It opened a fraction, and a few words were exchanged through the crack in low tones. Ogrin clicked his heels together, saluted, and started walking back to them.

"Your lucky day, my friend," he said to Belasko once he'd rejoined them. "Our master would like to meet you before he goes. I'm to take you to him now. Follow me."

"Who is your master? Which guard do you belong to?" Belasko asked as he followed the tall man down the corridor.

They drew up by the door and Ogrin rapped on it with his knuckles. He winked at Belasko. "You'll figure it out soon enough." The guard opened the door and indicated that Belasko should enter. "Maybe I'll see you again sometime."

"All right. Bye for now." Belasko turned and stepped through the door, Ogrin pushing it closed behind him.

Belasko entered Markus's study. The Royal Champion sat behind his desk, the remains of his evening meal spread out before him. A decanter of wine and some glasses, two of them used, sat on the desk. A finely dressed man with long dark hair just beginning to be streaked with grey occupied the chair opposite Markus. Hair that, Belasko couldn't help but notice, was held back by a golden circlet.

The figure stood as Belasko entered and turned to face him. Fine features with a sardonic cast to them lifted in a smile. "Ah, Belasko. A pleasure to meet you at last. You fought so well for me in the war with the Baskans. I, and all of Villan, owe you a great debt."

Although he had never seen him in the flesh, Belasko knew he was face to face with King Mallor, ruler of Villan.

Belasko sank to one knee. "Your majesty, the pleasure—the honour—is all mine."

"Nonsense. Do get up, you'll make the knees of your hose all baggy if you carry on like that." King Mallor held out a hand to him. "Please, get up."

Belasko took the offered hand and stood. The king pulled him closer, clasping Belasko's hand in both of his. "I mean what I say. Your actions at Dellan Pass were a significant blow to the Baskan war effort. You most likely shortened the war by at least a year, perhaps more, that day. I will find a way to reward you. It shames me it has taken this long."

Belasko shook his head. "No, majesty, I didn't act as I did or fight in the war for reward. It was the right thing to do, so I did it."

King Mallor laughed. "How simply he says it! He talks of holding a pass, alone, against far greater enemy numbers, as if it was the same as mending a wall or digging a ditch." He released Belasko's hand, taking him by the shoulders instead. "It is rare to meet a man who will do what is right, no matter the cost or difficulty it brings to himself. As I say, I'm honoured to meet you at last. But now I must go. I've monopolised enough of Markus's time. You must have your meeting."

Markus, who had stood when the king did, now moved around to the same side of the desk. "Majesty, thank you for paying me a visit. I hope I've reassured you as to our progress here—something I am just about to discuss with Belasko."

"Yes, you certainly have. Farewell for now, Markus, and you, Belasko. I have a feeling this is not the last time we will meet."

With that, the King of Villan nodded to both men, then opened the door and swept out of the room.

Belasko looked at Markus, blinking in not a little surprise. "Well," he said, "that was unexpected."

Markus laughed. "Don't worry. I think he likes you. Please, sit." He gestured to the chair only recently vacated by their sovereign and went back to his own side of the desk, retaking his seat.

Markus smiled at Belasko, the silver in his hair and beard gleaming in the lamplight, and gestured at the room. "Please, sit. Don't make me ask again." As Belasko pulled out the chair across from him, Markus reached for the decanter and another of the glasses set out on the tray on his desk. "Wine?" At a nod from Belasko, he poured, passing a glass over the table.

"Thank you." Belasko took a sip before making an appreciative face. "Very nice. Thank you again."

Markus waved away his thanks. "My pleasure."

Belasko drank more, taking a moment to appreciate the taste on his tongue before nodding at the dinner things that were scattered across the table. "Why don't you eat with the rest of us, instead of up here alone?"

Markus watched him over the rim of his glass for a moment before replying. "I thought the evening meal would be an excellent opportunity for all of you to bond as a group; to talk over the day's training. My presence there would be... disturbing."

"I see. That makes sense."

Markus gulped, taking a large mouthful of his wine. "I promise I won't keep you overlong. I just wanted to have a few words with you. As I've done with some of the others over the last few days."

"Oh," Belasko said, surprised. "Nobody's said anything about that."

"Because I've asked them not to. I'm only having these brief chats with those I see as most likely to be my successor." Markus took a more delicate sip of his wine. "Do you understand what I'm saying?"

Belasko's heart pounded in his chest, and he found his throat closed up, leaving him almost unable to speak. He shook his head. "You mean me—that is, you could choose me? As your successor?"

Markus laughed. "Yes, Belasko, that is what I mean. Why else are you here? But I wanted to talk to you and let you know more about what the role entails. What you must do to succeed."

Belasko nodded. "Yes, of course."

"First, let me ask you this: why do you want to be the Royal Champion?"

"It's something I never would have imagined." Belasko smiled slightly, shaking his head. "You have to understand, I grew up poor. Son of mountain farmers, scratching a life out of the dirt. Maybe some others here, the ones that attended fencing schools, whose families could afford that sort of thing, have dreamed of this all their lives. I ran away to join the army with visions of glory in my mind. Life has taken a few unexpected turns since then, but to be here—to be within touching distance of being the first commoner to be Royal Champion, of being an important figure at court. It's more than the young boy I was could have dreamed of. I just wanted to return to my village with a few good war stories, to impress the people I grew up amongst. This is something else entirely."

Markus smiled. "Well you've certainly earned more than your fair share of glory. I think those people would be impressed. You're here because of your reputation, which precedes you into any room. A hero of the Last War, your feats in battle... you've already taken the role of champion once, of course. At Dellan Pass. Though perhaps you didn't appreciate what it signified at the time."

"To be honest, I was just trying to stay alive. Buy enough time that my friend could return with every soldier he could find." He swallowed. "The things that happened that day, that have happened since... Well, I could never have imagined it." He shook his head. "Any of it."

"I'd be surprised if you had." Markus leaned forward. "Belasko, let me be frank. You are one of the most naturally gifted swordsmen I've ever met. Your speed and power..." He sighed. "I've rarely seen the like. Your technique needs some work. Some refining. But that's a matter of practice. You also possess something that I cannot teach, that can carry you through when skill and technique might fail. You have heart. There's an implacability to your fighting." Markus shifted in his seat. "I get the feeling that you would carry on the fight, no matter what, until your last breath. That would be an asset as Royal Champion and no mistake."

Belasko flushed at the praise from the older man. "I don't know about that. I fight the only way I know how."

Markus nodded. "Yes. However," he raised a finger, "there is more to the role of Royal Champion than being good with a blade, believe it or not. You would become a figure at court, have the ear of the king. You come from common stock. Am I right?"

"Yes, I'm a farmer's son."

Markus nodded. "That's what I thought. Ask yourself, are you prepared for that? To learn the courtly dances, which fork to use with which course. How to dress, how to act, how to carry yourself at court and in the company of royalty. Will you do that? *Can* you do that?"

Belasko was quiet for a moment, thinking before he answered. "I can do that."

"You might have to work on your presentation a bit. By which I mean, there is an element of performance to duelling. You might have to hide your humble nature under a little flamboyance." Markus laughed and sat back in his seat. "There is something else to consider. If you were to be my successor, it would mean dedicating yourself completely to the martial arts. You would need to be proficient with any weapon you care to name, and at unarmed combat. Dedicate yourself, excluding all else." He paused. "By this I mean, no family entanglements. No wife, no children. Nothing that could be used against you. Nobody for you to leave grieving should you lose. Know this: for a soldier, death is a possibility; for a duellist, it is an inevitability. Spare others their grief when you eventually come up against someone faster, someone better. Someone younger. Because it will happen."

Belasko opened his mouth to speak, but Markus held up a hand to stop him.

"No, don't say anything. Just think on what I've said, on what it would mean to become the Royal Champion. What you would be giving up as much as gaining. Go now, back to your room, and consider it." He grinned. "Feel free to take the wine with you."

Belasko stood. "Thank you, sir. I might take you up on that. There's just one thing. That life you speak of—a wife, children—has never been a consideration for me. I'm otherwise inclined, if you take my meaning."

Markus nodded. "I do. But that doesn't mean you won't have loved ones, a partner in life. Not all families are born, some are made. It's a lot to give up, no matter your inclinations. Take the wine and think on it. From tomorrow, things change, and I need to know that you're committed to this life."

❧

Belasko returned to his room, Markus's decanter in one hand and a wine glass in the other. To his surprise, Anerin was waiting outside his room. The young lord was holding a bottle of wine himself, and two cups. He arched his eyebrow when he saw what Belasko was carrying.

"I see you had the same idea. Shame you started without me."

Belasko laughed. "I was just with Markus. He wanted to see me about something. He offered me the decanter when I left. I thought it too good an opportunity, and too nice a wine, to pass up." He frowned. "Don't take this the wrong way, Anerin, but what are you doing here?"

Anerin shrugged. "I felt like some company, and thought it might be a suitable opportunity to, um, discuss some things we have in common."

"Things we have in common? You're an aristocrat; I'm a farmer's son. What could we have in common?"

Anerin had moved closer as Belasko spoke, close enough that Belasko could feel his breath. It was warm and had a faint fragrance of cloves. The young lord tilted his head to one side, looking deeply into Belasko's eyes. "I think we have at least one thing in common."

Belasko's heart fluttered in his chest, a nervous sensation he normally associated with going into battle. "Oh. I see. Well, yes, you might be right. It's just that, um..."

Anerin withdrew a little. "There's someone else?" he

asked. Belasko nodded. "And this someone, is he here? Does he return your feelings?"

Belasko shook his head. "No, on both counts. He can't return my feelings. He's not... He doesn't share our common interest. But that doesn't change the way I feel." He sighed. "In fact, he's getting married next month, and I'm to stand with him."

A sad smile worked its way onto Anerin's face. "Oh, Belasko. Mixing love or lust and friendship is always a dangerous game. I tell you what, let's have a cup of wine together, and you can tell me all about this man who's captured your heart. I promise not to seduce you."

Belasko laughed. "Very well then, if you promise. I think I'd like some company after all." He opened the door and entered his room. Anerin followed.

As they gathered the following morning for breakfast, Byrta and Belasko waited for Artur. And waited.

"He's not normally late coming down," said Byrta.

"Nor are this many of the others," said Belasko, looking around at the half-empty refectory. "Where is everybody? We're missing half of the students."

Apart from them, only eight others were in the refectory, all looking confused. They gathered around the long dining table. Ervan remained, as did Anerin and a few of the other students from wealthy backgrounds. Belasko and Byrta were the only remaining representatives of the Villanese military.

"Where have our fellow students got to?" asked Anerin as they took their seats.

"If they're not here, it must be for a reason. Did anyone check their rooms?" asked Belasko.

"Empty," said Ervan. "As if they went in the night. All of them. I suppose we'll find out why from Markus this morning. Gone they may be, but we need to focus. Stop worrying about them. Enjoy your breakfast."

Belasko and Byrta frowned at each other, but recognising some truth in Ervan's words, began to eat.

When they arrived in the training room a short while later, Markus was waiting for them.

"Come on, everyone, gather round. I suppose you're wondering where the rest of the students have gone?" He looked around at them, taking in the nods and enquiring looks, then sighed. "I'm afraid that they've all been sent home. Or back to their units. We find ourselves at a crucial point, near to the end of our endeavours here. The time will come, soon, when I will choose my successor, and those who have left us were... well, not up to the task. Those of you who remain, I feel you have it within you to be the next Royal Champion."

He paused, giving them all a meaningful look. "I have spoken to you all separately, given you time to think on just what that would mean. Anyone who thinks they don't have it in them, or who don't want it, can leave now without shame."

No one moved. Markus smiled. "Good. So we enter the last stage of our time here together—the final training before I make my choice. You will compete to help me decide. Victory alone will not be the deciding factor. Your conduct—*how* you fight—will also be a deciding factor. Good luck. You'll need it."

**4**

A few days later, the remaining students were summoned to the training room. Markus awaited them, stood at the front of the room with his hands behind his back. Once they had all filed in and formed up in front of him, he began to speak.

"Firstly, let me say that I am very proud of all of you. Among your number is the next Royal Champion—the one to stand at the king's side and protect his honour and that of the realm. Today is the day we have our little competition to help me choose just who that will be."

The students looked at each other, excited but unsure of what would be next. Markus continued, "We will replicate a formal duelling situation, with practice blades, and whoever has performed most admirably by the end, I will judge worthy of succeeding me." He held up a warning finger. "Remember, your conduct as well as your adaptability and suitability to the role will be taken into consideration." He clapped his hands. "Go perform any rituals you feel necessary to prepare yourselves. We begin here in one hour."

The students all filed out again, silent but eyeing up their opponents. This was it. This was the day it would be decided. At least one life would be changed forever.

~

Once they had all prepared themselves and convened once more in the duelling hall, Markus addressed them again.

"Today, we will do our best to replicate a formal duel. As we don't want anyone dead or injured too badly, we will continue with practice blades. You all know that duels are either fought to first blood, or to the death. I don't think in this instance either first blood or first touch will be sufficient. So we will fight to the first to three touches. If there is a clear break in movement following a touch, then the combatants will reset before commencing the next round. But don't forget: this is not a fencing match. This is a duel. Behave honourably but remember the swordsman's intent. Kill or be killed. Victory is all. You will all get the chance to duel each other over the course of the day. I've arranged a rotation that will give you all rest periods between bouts, but I encourage you to watch your fellow students. During a real duel there would be onlookers, often shouting encouragement or abuse, so please help replicate this environment. And don't hold back. You will draw lots to decide your initial opponents, then proceed on the rotation system." He paused, looking them all over, then smiled. "I'm proud of you to have made it to this point. All of you have grown in stature and ability over the last few weeks. Only one of you can succeed me as Royal Champion, but I hope you all take valuable lessons away with you from your time here. If you are successful, the really hard work starts tomorrow. Now, let's begin."

Belasko found himself paired with a student called Ravel, a whip-thin young man with dark hair and a serious expression. Their bout wasn't first up, so they watched the opening duels together. One of the earliest pairings to take to the circle were Byrta and Ervan. Byrta was good and quick, but Ervan was better and soon got the upper hand, besting her quite quickly. Belasko frowned as the pair left the circle, although he made sure to smile at Byrta when he caught her eye.

"She keeps dropping her shoulder," he said to Ravel. "It meant Ervan could get over her blade and inside her defences too easily. We've been working on it—I don't know why she's fallen back into old habits."

"You've been working together?" Ravel asked.

Belasko shrugged. "A few of the students. We decided we wanted a little extra practice to see what we could learn from each other. Markus approved."

"I wish I'd known about it. I could have done with a bit more training time."

"Sorry," said Belasko. "I need to talk to her. I'll be right back."

He went over to Byrta, who was stood in a corner muttering to herself as she swung her sword arm, stretching out.

"Hey," said Belasko, "how was that?"

"Pretty awful, or weren't you watching?" Byrta frowned. "I can't believe I lost to that little lordling."

"He's good. There's no shame in it. You kept dropping your shoulder though. I thought we'd worked on that?"

Byrta sighed. "I know, I know. I thought I'd ironed out that particular problem, but then... It's performing like this, in front of a crowd. I got nervous, and it crept back in."

"It's okay," said Belasko. "Just remember for your next

bout: the only thing that matters is your opponent and the blade in their hand. Try to ignore the crowd. Focus on your challenger and pretend no one else is here. It's different to a battle situation, where you need to keep your wits about you and focus on your surroundings as well. Here it's all about the two people in the circle, not a whole line of combatants. Or worse, a melee."

"You're right, I know it. I'll try."

Belasko clapped her on the shoulder. "You'll do better than that—you'll succeed. I know it."

Belasko's bout with Ravel came up shortly afterwards, and he dispatched his opponent with relative ease in just a few minutes.

As the two combatants bowed and left the circle, Ravel muttered to Belasko, "How did you get so fast? You've been good in training, very good, but that was something else."

Belasko shrugged. "That was practice. This is reality. Or at least, close to it. There's something about facing a real opponent that brings out my best."

Ravel stopped, staring at Belasko. "You mean, in training, that wasn't your best?"

Belasko laughed, clapping him on the shoulder. "Don't worry about it. You're warmed up now. You'll do better in your next match."

The day progressed, bout following bout, and although each fighter had a rest period between duels, tiredness soon began to show among the combatants. Only a few seemed unaffected—Belasko, Ervan, and Byrta among them.

"How are you three still so fresh?" Anerin gasped after one of his bouts. "I'm floundering like a dying fish after all this, and you seem like you just got out of bed."

Byrta shrugged. "A few years in his majesty's cavalry,

most of which were spent at war, will give you plenty of endurance."

"Likewise," said Belasko, "and I grew up working on my family farm, often from dawn until dusk. I had stamina before I joined the army."

Ervan smiled slyly. "I missed both of your advantages, having neither fought in a war nor toiled in the dirt. But I have been training for this," he pointed to the circle where Ravel and Bryn were engaged in furious combat, each striving to land a touch on the other, "my entire life."

"I'm good with a blade, there's no doubting that. But I don't think I'll be winning the ultimate prize today." Anerin shook his head. "I lack the dedication required."

"At least you're good company," said Byrta, grinning.

"There is that. Perhaps, when today is done, you can lead us on another tour of the city's more disreputable haunts?" Belasko asked, smiling.

"Just no stabbings this time, eh?" Byrta laughed. Anerin joined in, but Ervan's expression turned cold.

"If you'll excuse me, I need to warm up for my next duel," he said as he turned and stalked away.

"What's soured his milk?" asked Anerin, a puzzled look on his face.

"I don't know," said Belasko, "but don't let him put you off. We're all in with a chance today, no matter what you say, Anerin. Otherwise, we wouldn't be here. Let's keep our focus. We can arrange celebrations and commiserations later."

As the morning progressed, two clear leaders emerged: Ervan and Belasko. Both of whom seemed to have ascended to a separate plane in terms of ability and focus. By the time they faced each other, they were both undefeated, with only a few touches scored against them.

They entered the circle, bowing to each other and taking their positions. To Belasko, it was as if the rest of the world fell away. The sound of the others in the room became muted. Whatever was on the other side of the line marked out on the floor of the duelling hall faded into the distance, and all that was left was his opponent. Ervan. His sole focus. A slight sneer on his cold and distant features, no respect shown. No quarter would be given.

Markus called out to start, and they sprang into movement, warily circling each other.

By now, the pair had been training alongside and sparring with each other for weeks. They knew each other's habits and fighting styles, which Ervan was counting on.

Ervan's normal style was cautious, taking time to probe his opponent's defences. Instead, he leaped forwards, practice blade weaving in a glittering frenzy of furious movement as he threw himself across the circle. It was a glorious charge, and likely would have caught out a slower opponent, but Belasko kept his cool. He offered no defence and simply sidestepped Ervan's charge at the last moment, once the young courtier had committed to the move with all his body weight and momentum. He brought his blade around as he did so, catching Ervan a blow to his side as he passed.

"One touch to Belasko!" called Markus. The audience cheered, and Ervan looked furious, shooting Belasko a look of utter venom.

"A brave move, but foolhardy," said Belasko from across the circle. "In a real fight, you'd be nursing a gaping wound to your side."

Ervan shrugged, trying to appear nonchalant. "Good thing it's not a real fight. I can try again."

"Come on then. Let's see what else you have up your

sleeve." Belasko grinned at Ervan, an expression that was not returned as they retook their places.

This time it was Belasko that exploded into movement, launching a dazzling array of connected attacks, each flowing into the next as Ervan countered and held his own against the frenetic onslaught. They moved around the circle, Belasko pushing ever forwards, implacable, Ervan calmly meeting the attacks as he backed away. Biding his time to strike.

The time came as Belasko made a small mistake. He committed too deeply to a lunge, leaving his weight too far forward over his right knee. Ervan sidestepped the lunge, moved to the inside of Belasko's attack, and kicked his knee. Overbalanced, Belasko staggered forward out of the lunge, almost falling as he tried to bring his sword back around to protect himself. It was too late. Ervan's blade was quicker, stabbing Belasko in the gut and leaving him winded and gasping for breath.

"One touch to Ervan—combatants even!" called Markus. There was cheering and a smattering of applause from the other students, all of whom were enjoying the show.

"It's that technique of yours, Belasko. Still a little rough around the edges." Now it was Ervan's turn to grin.

Belasko nodded. "I know I've still plenty to learn," he called across the circle as they reset for the third round. "I won't make that mistake twice."

Ervan was cautious as the third round began, and again it was Belasko who attempted an audacious move. After a few tentative attacks, he seemed to commit himself to a high strike, bringing his sword down towards Ervan's head. As Belasko brought down his blade, Ervan went on the attack, swinging a vicious blow at Belasko's exposed side in an attempt to land a touch first. A futile move in a real duel, as it left him unprotected from Belasko's strike, but viable in this situation. However, as Ervan's blow came around, Belasko leaped and twisted, almost rolling his body over Ervan's blade. Ervan, fully committed to his swing, was pulled off balance as his blade met no resistance. He could only watch as Belasko completed his twisting leap, bringing his blade around in a low sweep as he landed in a crouch, striking the back of Ervan's legs. His knees buckled, and he fell forwards, carried by his own momentum.

As Ervan fell to his knees, Belasko spun around and planted a boot square in the middle of his back, pushing him over. Ervan landed on his front, sprawling, practice sword falling from his hand. Belasko's boot pinned him to the ground. He brought his blade to bear and rested the point gently on the back of Ervan's head.

"I make that three touches to me," said Belasko, chest heaving with exertion. "What does the referee say?"

Markus stroked his chin as he contemplated, replaying the last round in his mind. "Ordinarily, we would expect to reset to opening positions after a touch. However, in this instance, I consider both touches part of the same move, and so I'll allow it." He held up his hand. "Three touches— Belasko wins!"

Belasko lifted his boot from Ervan's back, releasing him. As the young courtier rolled onto his back, Belasko offered a hand to help him stand. Ervan batted it away, struggling to his feet on his own. His face was dark with fury.

"No!" he shouted. "That last move, that—that was dishonourable. To hit an opponent in the back, striking them when they're down. It's not right."

Markus stepped into the ring, approaching them both.

"That last move," he said, quietly, "was a piece of balletic genius, the likes of which I've never seen. Dishonourable? Ervan, do you think that in a real duel your opponent will give you time to get back on your feet? Offer you a hand up? Never forget the swordsman's intent. Kill or be killed. No, the move stands. Belasko wins this bout."

Ervan looked like he was about to object again, but caught the warning look on Markus's face and instead gave a strangled noise of frustration as he stalked out of the circle.

Markus clapped Belasko on the shoulder. "That was well done, Belasko. I'm very impressed." He turned back to the audience. "Next bout!" he called.

The day continued, but the mood was soured.

The competition ended with several students having outperformed the rest, Ervan and Belasko highest amongst them. They all gathered around Markus, who stood in the centre of the duelling circle. They were tired after the many hours of training, the long day of duelling, but most of those who had lost were happy, having given their all. Most, but not all. Markus began to speak.

"I'm proud of you. All of you. You should be proud of yourselves. You have trained hard, fought well, given all that I asked of you and more. You are all deserving in your own ways. However, I can choose only one of you to be my successor."

He looked around at the group, the hopeful expressions on some faces, resignation on others.

"The person I choose has been exemplary throughout their time here. Not just in their sword work, but in their attitude. Their conduct. They have demonstrated to me, in many ways, that they are the right choice to be my successor. To train with me, and one day soon, to take on the mantle of the Royal Champion. Defender of the king's own honour."

He paused, then smiled. "Fittingly, it is a role he has taken on before, albeit by happenstance. Belasko, I choose you."

Belasko blinked, surprised, before a slow smile spread across his face. The other students surrounded him, clapping him on the shoulder, on the back, calling out congratulations. All save one: Ervan, who stood apart, face expressionless, cold, like a statue hewn from marble.

Markus walked over to Belasko and held out his hand, which the younger man gripped and shook.

"Thank you, Markus, sir. It's an honour. I'll do my best to repay your faith in me," said Belasko. "I—"

"No," said Ervan. The others quieted, looking at the young aristocrat with puzzled expressions. "No," he said again, "it can't be. He cannot be the champion."

Markus's expression was frosty. "Why not? Who are you to say, to dictate my choice?"

"I'm better than him—than all of you. It should be me."

"Ervan, I'm sorry you're upset," said Belasko, "but there was only ever going to be one of us chosen. Most of the people in this room were going to be disappointed today. I fully expected to be. This surprises me as much as anyone, but—"

"Surprise?" Byrta snorted. "You've been the best of us the whole way through this. I'm definitely not surprised. Almost relieved it's not me, to be honest." She grinned at Belasko. "Sounds like a lot of work."

Ervan's eyes were fixed on Belasko. "I can beat you."

"You've not managed it so far—not in training, and not today. What makes you so convinced?" Markus's voice was as cold as his expression. "No. You've had your chance and are now embarrassing yourself, dishonouring me and the others present. I think you should withdraw your comments and think a little more carefully before speaking in future."

"I challenge!" Ervan called out, voice ringing like a bell. "I challenge Belasko. One last bout, one last duel to decide the matter."

"You forget yourself, boy. I decide the matter!" snapped Markus.

Belasko held up a hand for silence. "No, it is his right. If he feels he has no option but to challenge, I accept."

"Very well, but practice blades only. Clear the circle!" Markus's expression was becoming angrier by the moment. His face was flushed, and a vein on his temple was more and more pronounced.

"Practice blades?" Ervan scoffed. "Surely the hero of Dellan Pass isn't afraid of a live blade?"

Markus whirled around to face him. "*He* isn't. I just have no desire to send you back to your mother in a pine box. If you fought with live blades, that would be the only conclusion."

Ervan sneered. "I think differently. Come on then, Belasko, with practice blades."

The others cleared the circle while Ervan and Belasko retrieved their blades from where they had been set aside only a short while ago. As they took up their positions across from each other, Markus strode into the centre of the circle.

"Same rules as the competition, except first touch wins. And Ervan, this decides nothing but the level of your embarrassment. Ready?" The combatants took up their stances. "Good. You may begin as soon as I have left the circle."

As he left the boundary marked on the floor, Ervan launched a lightning-fast strike, which Belasko deflected, and the fight was on.

Ervan threw himself into the bout like never before, fully committed, desperate to beat Belasko. Belasko countered his every move with astonishing speed and deadly efficiency whilst seeming totally at ease. They almost danced around each other, around the circle, but it was a dance designed to catch the other party out. Their blades, though they were dulled for practice, wove a dazzling web of steel.

This continued on, neither gaining more ground than they lost, until finally, Ervan made a small mistake. He put too much force into parrying one of Belasko's attacks, which left him open for a fraction of a second—a gap Belasko was not shy about exploiting. He threw himself forward in a lunge, the dulled tip of his practice blade touching Ervan's chest. The blade bent with the force of the blow as it caught in Ervan's clothing.

In that moment, time seemed to slow for the two combatants. Belasko continued to push forward with the force of his blow, deep in his lunge, when his blade gave a fragile, almost crystalline, sad little sound, and the metal snapped.

The tip of the blade fell to the ground as Belasko, weight fully committed, fell forwards. He desperately tried to pull his blow, but the now deadly sharp blade in his hands leaped up, released from where it had been caught in Ervan's clothing, and plunged directly into Ervan's right eye.

Now there was screaming. There was blood.

A few days after the accident Belasko, Anerin, and Byrta, who had been granted a few days' additional leave from her squadron, went to Ervan's family home to visit him. Information was scarce, but they knew he was convalescing there. As they approached the formidably large townhouse, Byrta whistled.

"I knew he came from money, but damn."

It was less a house and more of a complex, based around a large courtyard set back from a gated entrance to the street. There were even household guards stationed at the gates.

Anerin nodded. "Ervan's family is one of the wealthiest in the city. Their land and titles go far back, to the earliest days of the kingdom."

As they approached the gate, one of the guards stepped out to meet them, a halberd resting casually on his shoulder. Belasko could tell from the way he moved that he, and his halberd, could switch from casual to deadly in but a moment. The guard eyed them, taking in their attire, whilst his colleague lowered his matching halberd to block the entrance.

"All right, I'll bite," said the first guard. "What's your business here?"

Anerin, as the closest to Ervan's station, spoke first. "We're friends of Ervan's—been training with him, you see —and we thought we'd visit and see how he's getting on. Since the, um, accident."

The guard peered at him, taking in his fine clothing, and nodded. "You're welcome to come in this way, sir, and speak to Lady Lavinia—although I doubt you'll find her in a receptive mood. The others," he nodded at Belasko and Byrta in their military uniform and simpler attire, "will have to use the servants' entrance, round the back." Byrta bristled and was about to speak, but the guard got in first. "Not my choice, you understand. Just household policy."

Belasko put a hand on Byrta's arm. "Peace, friend, we'll go in whichever door will get us to see Ervan. Round the back, you say?"

The guard nodded. "That's right, sir, by where they empty the privies."

Anerin shook his head, a distasteful look spread across his face. "Thank you for the kind invitation to use the front door. However, we are here as a group. If my friends must be sent to the servants' entrance, we all go to the servants' entrance. Whether it's where the privies are emptied or not. Would you be so kind as to let Lady Lavinia know that we are calling?"

"Yes, sir. Very good, sir." The guard stepped back into his alcove by the gate, pulling on a cord that set a bell to ringing somewhere unseen. "I'll let one of the footmen know, sir."

As the group made their way around the side of the complex, past the rather fragrant area described, Anerin shook his head. "I know I'm considered posh, but I'd never send visitors to the servants' entrance. No matter who they were." He glanced at Belasko and Byrta. "No offence intended."

"No offence taken," said Byrta baldly. "None at all."

Anerin winced, and they continued the rest of their short journey in silence. When they reached the servants' entrance, a small and unremarkable door, they found a footman waiting.

"Please come in," he said. "The Lady Lavinia will see you in one of the receiving rooms."

He led them in through what seemed to be a storeroom of some kind, through the hot and noisy kitchens busy preparing the midday meal, and a confusing network of corridors, to a small room with a few chairs. Everywhere was opulent luxury. The corridors were festooned with decorative scrollwork, dripping with gold leaf. There were occasional tables with expensive-looking ceramics and silver at every turn. Even this modest room contained more wealth than Belasko had ever seen contained in one place. One of the chairs was occupied by Lady Lavinia, who did not stand to greet them.

"I won't ask you to sit," said Lady Lavinia, "for you won't be staying long."

"My dear Lady Lavinia," said Anerin, bowing his head respectfully. "I hope we haven't troubled you. We came to enquire after Ervan's health, and perhaps to see him if he's well enough. We are his friends, and have been training with him these last few weeks—"

"Friends?" Lady Lavinia scoffed. "I doubt that very much. Would friends have injured him so?"

"My lady," said Belasko, stepping forward. "What happened was an accident. A terrible, unfortunate accident. No one here wished Ervan any harm."

Now Lady Lavinia stood. "You dare?" she hissed at Anerin, refusing to address Belasko directly. "You dare bring him here? The one who harmed my son?" She pointed at Belasko, turned towards him. "Oh yes, I know who you are. Mark me well, boy. For what you have done to my son, for what you have taken from him, you will pay." She was shouting now. "You will pay! Now get out, all of you! Get out and never come here again!"

Ervan stirred, woken by some commotion that drifted up to his room from downstairs. He gave a little smile at the thought of whoever was on the receiving end of his mother's wrath, then winced. Any movement of his face was still painful. He had been drifting in and out of consciousness for the last few days, carried forward on the wave of a fever that had now broken. He felt tired, weak, in pain, but very much alive.

The door to his room opened, admitting his mother. "Oh, dear boy, did that wake you?" she asked. Lavinia moved to his bedside, stroking the side of his face that was not bandaged.

"It's all right, Mother. I was just feeling sorry for whichever of the servants had inspired your anger," he said, his voice croaking and weak.

She shook her head. "Not one of the servants." She sniffed. "Just some passing tradesmen that dared to call on me personally. I sent them on their way in no uncertain terms. Are you hungry? Would you like some food sent up?"

Ervan nodded and winced again. "Yes please, but something light. Soup, perhaps?"

"A nourishing broth, that's what you need. To build your strength. I'll have cook send some up in a moment. First, we need to talk about your future."

"My future? I'll be all right once I'm healed, and these are off." Ervan gestured to the side of his face that was swathed in bandages. "Then I can get back to training, compete to be Markus's successor."

"Ervan, my dear, Markus has already chosen his successor. That commoner," she almost spat the word. "Belasko. The one who did this to you."

"Belasko? Already? And did what, Mother? What

happened? What's wrong with my eye? The pain..." Ervan's hand drifted up towards his face again.

Lavinia took hold of his hand in both of hers and took a deep breath. "Son... The surgeons, they had to remove your eye. The damage was too severe for it ever to heal and it risked infection. As it was, the fever that struck after you took your wound nearly carried you off. No, I'm afraid your duelling days are done."

"What? I... but I... Mother, I don't know anything else. If I can't duel, if I can't fight, then what am I to do? What has been the point of all this?" He was crying now, from his one good eye. "The years of training, of pushing myself to be the best, and now this? Some commoner takes the place that should be mine? What am I to do?"

"Hush, child," she said, stroking his cheek. "I have been thinking. There are other ways to serve, ways in which your singularity of purpose could be redirected. My cousin, Vydan, he has need of good men in the Inquisition. Your breeding and connections would guarantee you a good rank."

"The Inquisition? Mother, I—"

"Peace, Ervan, peace. You're tired. Let me get that broth sent up, and we can talk again when you're stronger." She stood, casting a critical eye over him, then sniffed. "That hair will have to go. With a patch over your injury..." Lavinia smiled. "Yes, you'll make quite the terrifying Inquisitor. You mark my words. Then, one day, when the opportunity arises, we'll have our revenge on that common swordsman. Oh, yes. And it will be glorious."

She left the room. Ervan stared at his bedroom ceiling.

"The Inquisition," he murmured to himself, sleep already reaching back up to claim him. "Well, I've always looked good in black."

The End

To find out what revenge Ervan has in store for Belasko, make sure to pick up The Swordsman's Lament! Read on to sample the first two chapters.

# THE SWORDSMAN'S LAMENT - PREVIEW

## G.M. WHITE

G.M. WHITE

# THE
# SWORDSMAN'S
# LAMENT

## THE ROYAL CHAMPION : BOOK ONE

1

It was a little after lunch, and Belasko had already killed three men. He frowned at their bodies, scattered across the duelling circle which had been crudely scratched into the dirt of the street. He should have expected that his challenger had friends that wanted in on the act, but didn't expect them to break the rules and jump in all at once. Was nothing sacred anymore?

He touched his brow. It was as he'd said inside; he'd killed them without breaking a sweat. He flexed his foot. It was the damnable ache that slowed him, made his thrusts weaker, as he couldn't push off properly. These three, these boys, had got closer than anyone should, and all because of the pain in his foot. He sighed before turning to wave at the gathered crowd. He really was getting older.

Thirty-seven wasn't old by the standards of Villanese society, but it was old for a duellist. You don't see many old duellists, or retired ones, because there will always come someone who wants to challenge you. To build their reputation on your own. Worse still for the king's champion. No shortage of challengers for him.

*All I wanted was a bite to eat and some peace and quiet,* Belasko thought, *not to kill three stupid boys. Still, it was a damn fine meal...* He snorted. *And I thought I wouldn't be recognised in this part of town.*

❧

Belasko nursed his beer and looked around the inn. It was busy, a mix of people from different classes filling the public dining and taproom. Labourers dressed in rough cloth jostled for space on communal benches, whereas prosperous merchants paid extra for private tables. It was a middling sort of place, but he preferred those to the finer establishments the city had to offer. Less chance of recognition and the challenges that often followed. Still, the meal had been surprisingly good and the ale was very fine. When the innkeeper brought his bill, he tried to guess the worth of the food and drink he had just enjoyed.

He smiled at the older man, a stout fellow who was greying at the temples. An honest face hovered above the innkeeper's uniform of sturdy work clothes covered by an ever-present apron, shirtsleeves rolled up to the elbow, the harried look of the permanently busy about him. Belasko smiled and covered the bill with his hand.

"Now, my good man, before I look at the bill you've brought me, let me tell you that that was as fine a meal as I've eaten in any establishment in this city — and I've eaten at some of the very best. Before I leave, may I pay my compliments to the chef?"

The innkeeper coloured at the praise. "Kendra!" he bellowed over his shoulder before turning to smile at Belasko. "Thank you, sir, that is praise indeed. I know she's a good cook and all—"

They were interrupted by a young woman who came bustling out of the kitchens, wiping her hands on her apron. "What is it? If it's another—" She stopped short at the sight of Belasko and the smiling innkeeper. "Oh, sorry. How can I be of assistance?"

The innkeeper gestured at Belasko. "The gentleman here was just being very complimentary about the food and asked to meet the chef before he leaves."

"Kendra, was it? I..." Belasko paused, noticing the similarities between the innkeeper and the cook. "Your daughter?" he asked the innkeeper, who nodded. "You must be very proud. Kendra, the meal I have just eaten was simply delicious. The seasoning both delicate and exquisite. You have a rare gift." He looked at the innkeeper. "I must say, the beer is very fine too."

Belasko tapped his fingers on the bill the innkeeper had brought him. "Here's what I'd like to do. I'll put down what I think the meal is worth before I look at the bill. If the bill is for less, you keep the difference with my compliments; if it is higher then accept my apologies, and I'll reach into my purse again."

The innkeeper frowned but nodded, clearly unsure.

"Now, as I said, that was as fine a meal as I've eaten in this city, and I've eaten in establishments both low and high. I've dined at the palace on more than one occasion. Elsewhere in the city, I would happily pay, oh, four crowns and a stag." He laid the coins out on the table. The innkeeper's face paled at the sight of the money. "Now let's look at the bill." Belasko turned it over, read the amount written, and laughed. He slid the coins over to the innkeeper. "You, sir, are seriously undercharging. Please, take these with my compliments."

While the innkeeper and his daughter blushed at the

praise, and insisted that he accept the change he was due, Belasko smiled. He liked to tip generously when he could, and the meal really had been that good.

His purse strings were a little tighter than normal, having taken a loan to acquire more land for the academy. They needed better access to water and their own logging rights if they were to get through another winter as fierce as the last. Some wondered why a man at his station in life would resort to a loan, but while Belasko's star rode high in Villanese society, he put most of his money into the Academy and his students. When all was said and done, they were his legacy.

"No, no, please take the money. The meal was worth it. You really need to start charging more. Be careful, though. I hear the palace is looking for a new cook and they might poach Kendra right out from under you. If I didn't have a good cook on my staff already I know I'd be tempted."

Belasko was interrupted by a heavy hand on his shoulder. *Bugger. Recognised. Here it comes.*

"Here, ain't you that duellist? Greatest swordsman in the world or some shit?"

He stood and turned, chair screeching against the flagstones, throwing the hand off his shoulder and pushing back the man it belonged to in one smooth motion.

"Am I Belasko, most gifted with a blade? Hero of Dellan Pass? Never defeated in the duelling circle? The king's personal champion? Yes. Greatest swordsman in the world? I've yet to meet better, but in truth it's a young man's game and I'm no longer young."

"You don't look that old either," Kendra said from over his shoulder.

Belasko smiled at her. "That's very kind of you, but every

year I get a little slower, relying more on skill, technique and experience than speed. I've yet to meet my better, but one day that will come." He pursed his lips and eyed the young man that had recognised him, taking in his ragged clothing, the sword at his hip that although worn and battered through use, looked ill cared for. "But I think it is not today."

The rest of the inn, which had gone deathly silent at the prospect of a challenge, stirred into laughter at this. The man who had accosted Belasko flushed.

*Good. Anger. Anything that will put you out of balance,* Belasko thought. He turned to the room.

"Mind you, have you lot not heard the swordsman's lament?"

"No," came a voice from the crowd, "what's that?"

Belasko grinned. "The older I get, the better I was."

The crowd laughed louder at this and Belasko turned again to the man who had recognised him. "Are you sure you'd like to put me to the test, sir? While I might be getting older—" He flexed his left foot in his boot. The pain wasn't too bad today. "—I could still kill you and any other man in here without breaking a sweat." He smiled apologetically at the innkeeper and his daughter. "Not that I would. I would hate to spoil a very pleasant afternoon, or do any damage to your establishment. If this young idiot insists on throwing his life away, we'll take it outside."

He looked back at the man he knew he'd soon be fighting, noting that his insults had hit home. Belasko sighed and rolled his shoulders, freeing them up for what was to come.

"So, what is it to be? Will you challenge, or can I go back to enjoying my afternoon in peace?"

The young man drew himself up to his not unimpressive height. *Damn, he's tall. He'll have a better reach than me.* He sneered at Belasko, hawked and spat on the inn floor. "I challenge," he hissed from between his teeth.

Belasko sighed, before reaching into his purse and flicking another coin to the innkeeper. "Please, for the young man's rudeness and the inconvenience."

The innkeeper swallowed. "Inconvenience? When word gets out that Belasko fought a duel outside, our business will double."

Belasko smiled. "Then I wish you well of it." He turned back to his challenger, who had somehow managed to flush darker still and was almost purple with rage. "Oh yes, you. I accept. Shall we go outside?"

*Ah well, another tale to add to the legend. By the time the story of this afternoon's little adventure has spread three streets away, the number of attackers will have doubled. By the time it's reached the next quarter, they'll have tripled.*

Belasko leaned down, wiping the blood from his blade on the shirt of his fallen challenger before sheathing it in the scabbard he wore at his hip. A rapier, light and ideal for duelling, he always wore it about town.

"Excuse me, Mr Belasko? Sir?" Belasko looked up. It was the innkeeper.

Belasko smiled and clapped him on the shoulder. "Just Belasko is fine, and apologies again for this incident. It's a hazard of my trade I'm afraid. I'm sorry, I didn't take your name?"

The innkeeper blinked. "Kander, sir — I mean, Belasko. My name is Kander."

"Kander. I am sorry about this mess outside your establishment. No doubt the constables are already on their way to clear up. Ah, here they come now." The sounds of whistles in the distance heralded the arrival of the city watch. Belasko would apologise to them when they arrived, both for the mess and for having them stirred from their watch house.

Kander smiled. "Please, don't apologise. If people don't know better than to challenge the king's champion then they deserve what they get." He frowned. "Particularly when they break the rules of the circle. I couldn't believe it when the other two jumped in. That would never have happened in my day." The innkeeper shook his head. "A sign of the times."

"Your day? Were you a duellist?" *I should have known, he carries himself well.*

Kander laughed. "Oh no, sir — I mean, Belasko — not a duellist. I was a soldier in another life and we occasionally settled differences in the circle. Just to first blood, or they'd have had us hanged."

"That sounds like the wisdom of commanding officers: 'If you kill each other we'll hang you!' I was a soldier myself before — well, you know."

"I do. We all do. I doubt there's anyone in the country that doesn't know your story. Listen, can I offer you a drink? On the house. You've already overpaid for your meal, I couldn't charge you more."

Belasko looked around at the dispersing crowd. The street was already returning to its normal background hubbub, people taking care not to disturb the duelling circle and the bodies within as they made their way past and in and out of the nearby businesses. He shook his head. "I'd love to, Kander, but once word gets out about this challenge others will come. More idiots looking to make their mark. I'd best be getting home."

"I understand." Kander squinted at Belasko. "What you said before, about the palace kitchens, them needing a chef. Is that true? Only..." The innkeeper sighed. "My Kendra's too good for the inn. I can't charge what her food's worth, not in this part of town, and although it would hurt me to lose her I just want the best for my girl. She deserves her chance to shine. To show what she can do."

Belasko nodded. "It's true, and from what I've sampled she'd be more than up to the task. Would you like me to have a word, put her name forward?"

"Oh, if you could, that would be wonderful. Thank you!"

"In fact, I'll do better than that. Do you by any chance have private dining rooms?"

"Oh yes, several."

"Well, keep the grandest one you have free for me tomorrow night. I'll return to sample her cooking with some people who are best placed to make the decision. Just don't let on to anyone that I'm coming back, or that I'm bringing guests with me. Can you do that?"

Kander grinned. "Can I? Of course I can! Thank you so much, I honestly can't thank you enough. Oh, can I tell Kendra? Just so she can make something special."

"Of course, but no one else. Keep it secret, alright? We'll come to the back door, so as not to advertise our presence." Belasko reached out his hand and the two men clasped wrists, shaking on the deal.

"You know what's responsible for too much death? More than you'd think?" Maelyn, the royal physician, looked up from her examination of Belasko's left foot. A diminutive woman with steel grey hair, a fierce intelligence shone out of her piercing blue eyes. Her slight build belied a surprising strength.

"No, but I'm sure you'll enlighten me."

The next day found Belasko in the physician's suite at the palace, her treatment room to be precise. It was a functional room with several couches and treatment tables, the charts and illustrations of human anatomy hung on the walls the only decoration. A faint aroma from the remedies Maelyn prepared and dispensed hung in the air. He was stripped to his smallclothes sitting on a low couch, as Maelyn examined his bad foot and other joints.

"Pride. Damnable, pig-headed pride. Whether that's the pride that brings armies to battle—" Belasko winced as the physician probed the joints of his foot. "—or the pride that keeps someone from visiting their doctor so they then die of a curable illness. That last one is usually the preserve of men. You're from farming stock, aren't you? They're often the worst. Work themselves into the grave while their body falls apart, but mustn't grumble. Mustn't complain. Right." The little physician sat back and clapped her hands. "On with your clothes."

"So, what do you think?" Belasko asked as he shrugged on his shirt.

Maelyn's eyebrows rose. "What do I think? I think you have a problem that's not going to get any better."

Belasko reached for his breeches. "I know that, but will it get worse?"

The little physician sighed. "Yes, I'm afraid so. There are a few things you can do that should alleviate the pain and stiffness in your other joints, but I'm afraid the damage to your foot is permanent. It will only get worse. You've pushed your body hard over the years, and it's coming back to haunt you. It's rare to see such ailments in someone your age, but not unheard of. Tell me, have either of your parents had similar problems?"

"I don't know. I haven't seen them in years."

"I see."

Belasko cleared his throat. "What can I do, then? Anything?"

Maelyn pursed her lips. "You're already doing most of what can be done. Exercise is good, gets the blood flowing, and you do plenty of that. Try to keep to things that won't place too much impact on the joints — that's probably how you got into this state in the first place. Swimming is good, particularly in cold water. I think you said you had somewhere suitable on the grounds of your academy?"

Belasko nodded. "Yes, there's a small lake. More of a large pond, really. It's deep enough for swimming, bloody cold too."

"Good. Try to swim in it regularly. Avoid exercises that will jar your joints, such as, oh I don't know, banging bloody great lengths of steel together."

"Nice try. You know I can't do that. I need to keep training, both for my students and my own sake. I still get challenged, you know."

Maelyn frowned. "Yes, I heard about your little adventure yesterday. What was it, three at once?"

"It was only supposed to be one, then his friends joined in."

The physician sighed. "You no doubt dispatched them with style and aplomb. Let me ask you, though: how close did they get? I heard it was three unschooled boys that should have known better. How close?"

Belasko paused in the act of pulling on one of his boots. Then, quiet, "Too close. They got too close."

Maelyn leaned over and patted him on the shoulder.

"You might be the best, my boy, but age comes to us all. There's no harm in getting out while you still can. Why not retire?"

"Don't you know, Doctor, there are no retired duellists? Only dead ones." Belasko shook his head. "Besides, I can't retire yet. I've too much to do. A replacement to find and train up."

"And how long have you been looking, my boy? How many years? You'll not find another like you. You're a rare breed. A legend, or so they tell me. You might just have to settle for someone that can do the job."

"When I find someone who can do the job as well as I can, that's when I'll retire."

The physician laughed. "I'll believe it when I see it. Now, off with you. I'll make up something to help with the pain in your foot and have it sent over to your house. Where are you off to now?"

Belasko stood, straightening his collar. "I have dinner plans."

Across town, Kander was fretting around his daughter in the kitchen. A hot, busy room, clouds of steam and the smell of cooking food filled the air. With staff bustling in and out, Kendra ruled over the kitchen from her position between the ovens and the open fireplace. She frowned, swatting her father's hands away from a cooking pot with a wooden spoon.

"Come now, Father, there's no need to be nervous. The duellist already said he liked our food. What more do we have to prove?"

Kander wrung his hands, uncharacteristically anxious.

"It's just the people he's bringing with him, they'll decide whether you get taken on at the palace kitchens. Isn't that something to be nervous about?"

Kendra gave her father a stony look. "You know I'm happy here. If these guests are impressed by my cooking and offer me a job at the palace, then that's wonderful. If they don't, that's fine too. It's not like I've lost anything if I don't get offered the job. Besides, who'll look after little Albin if I go up to the palace?" Her son, at five years old, was a handful. Between Kendra, her father, and the other staff at the inn, they managed to care for him and keep him mostly out of trouble. As she looked at her father her expression softened and she leaned forward to place a kiss on his brow. "I suppose we'll sort things out if it comes to that. Now look, you fretting in here is putting me off. Let me get on with what I do best, and you get ready to welcome our guests. And make sure not to forget about our regulars in the common room in the process."

Kander threw his hands up. "Alright, alright, I know when I'm not wanted." He winked at her to soften his words. "I'll go and busy myself in the common room until they arrive."

He went out, leaving Kendra to her work. She frowned, tapping a finger on her lips. "Now, where did I put that Aruvian pepper?"

As they approached the back door to the inn, Belasko murmured to his companions, "Best let me knock and exchange pleasantries before we go in. We don't want our little escort to alarm anyone."

He walked down the back street accompanied by three

figures, all cloaked and hooded against the evening's chill, and a small company of guards in plain livery but well-made armour — functional, not flashy. Belasko himself was dressed in well-made doublet and hose in muted colours, careless of the increasing cold, with a short cape thrown nonchalantly over one shoulder to leave his sword arm free, and knee-high riding boots on his feet. Their footsteps clattered on the cobbles and echoed off the surrounding buildings, mingling with the occasional clink of armour and creak of leather, before being lost in the general hubbub of the city at night.

The taller of the three hooded forms waved his hand in the air. "Whatever you say Belasko, I'm sure we're happy to follow your lead. Just let's not be too long about supper, I have a function I need to get to later this evening."

A snort came from under one of the other's hoods, followed by a wry voice. "A 'function', is it? Another one of your revelries I'm sure. Still, if the food Belasko's promised us is as good as he says then you'll be well set up for an evening of carousing."

The third, shortest and slight of build, remained silent.

*Once again I play the mediator.* "Come now gentlemen, no need for argument. Let us enjoy our dinner. Debate is best made on a full stomach. Over brandy. Ah, here we are." Belasko stepped up to the stout back door of the inn, the muted sounds of its inhabitants and their own evening's revelries drifting down to them from high windows. He rapped firmly on the door three times.

There followed a few quiet moments, then the sound of bolts being thrown back before the door was heaved open and Kander, blinking out at the dark, stood before them.

"Belasko! Welcome, welcome. You're just in time. Do come in."

Belasko reached out and clasped the inn keeper's hand. "Good to see you again, Kander. Do you mind if a few of our men have a quick look inside first? Just to check the dining room, you understand."

Kander peered out, taking in Belasko's companions and retinue. He swallowed. The number of guards and the quality of their armour spoke volumes about the wealth and importance of the guests he would be hosting. "Of—of course I don't mind. Please, gentlemen, this way. Let me show you through to the dining room, it's the finest we have..." Kander's voice faded as he led several of the guards down the corridor.

"Tell me, what do we know of this innkeeper?" asked Belasko's second companion, their wry tone replaced with curiosity.

Belasko shrugged. "Once a soldier, seems a good sort. His daughter is an exceptionally talented cook. What more do you need to know?"

His companion laughed. "You would never have made an intelligence operative, Belasko. There's always more to any situation than meets the eye, and I like to know as much as I can about the people I meet."

Belasko grinned, patting the rapier at his side. "It's a good thing you don't keep me around for my intelligence then, isn't it?"

All his companions laughed at this, the tallest reaching out to clap him on the shoulder. "Never mind old man, you have many redeeming qualities, I'm sure. Do let us know when you find out what they are."

Belasko raised an eyebrow. "'Old man'? Less of that, if you please. I'm only a few years older than you and could still best you every day of the week, twice on feast days ."

His third companion spoke at last, a female voice.

"Really gentlemen, is this what passes for wit in the company of men? I should have stayed at home with my books, at least they're reliably entertaining."

They all laughed again just as their guard returned with Kander. They nodded, apparently satisfied with the arrangements inside.

"Right then," Belasko said, pointing at guards as he spoke, "two of you stay out here to mind the door, two come to watch the stairs — the dining room is upstairs, isn't it Kander?" The inn keeper nodded. "Good. Two more to guard the door to the dining room. The rest of you, disperse but don't go far. Keep an eye on the entrances and exits. It might be an idea to have a few men in the common room, but watch what you drink. You're still on duty."

The guardsmen peeled off to their assignments and Belasko and his companions followed Kander into the inn.

The innkeeper led them into a sumptuously decorated private dining room, with deep carpets and intricately detailed tapestries on the walls. The furniture was expensive, dark hard wood polished until it gleamed, and there were curios and decorations of excellent craftsmanship on stands and in cabinets around the walls. Pride of place was given to the large dining table and chairs in the centre of the room.

Belasko whistled. "Kander, you surprise me. This is fine indeed."

Kander shrugged. "I know we might not be in the best part of town, but I like to aim high. Word of Kendra's skill in the kitchen has got around. We get the occasional noble or lord merchant coming to dine. Might as well make them feel welcome."

One of Belasko's companions moved to the table, where four places were set, and took the place at its head. "Never mind nobles or lord merchants my good Kander, I'd say your dining room is fit for a king." He drew back the hood of his cloak, revealing himself to be a fine-featured older man, with salt and pepper beard and hair, and a sardonic smile. Clad in a black and gold brocade doublet, richly embroidered with the royal house's silver stag, a gold circlet sat on his brow.

The taller companion, at his right hand side, drew back his own hood. "And maybe for his son as well." A handsome man in his early thirties, he had dark hair, the flushed complexion of a seasoned drinker, and a self-satisfied grin. His doublet was equally fine, of scarlet and gold, depicting satyrs chasing dancing nymphs. He wore a silver circlet.

"Let's not forget his daughter, shall we?" At this the third companion drew back her hood, revealing herself to be a young woman, fine featured with golden hair that was artfully entwined around her own silver circlet. She wore a gown of deceptively simply cut, with white and gold panels, tightly laced across the bodice and trimmed with fur at the cuffs and hems. A playful smile hovered about her lips, threatening to break out at any time.

Kander gawped at the three of them.

*As different as they make out they are, they all enjoy this sort of thing,* Belasko thought. "Well," he said aloud, "I did tell you I'd bring people who were best placed to decide who gets employed in the palace kitchens. Who better than the most important people that would be eating the food?"

Kander swallowed, gathered himself, and offered a deep bow. First to the man wearing the gold circlet, then the man and woman in silver. "King Mallor, your majesty. Your highnesses Prince Kellan, Princess Lilliana, I had no idea… My humble house is honoured. I'm sorry, Belasko didn't tell me…"

King Mallor smiled gently. "Peace, honourable innkeeper. It is good that he didn't. We have to keep such excursions outside the palace walls quiet, for safety's sake."

"Also we'll get a much more honest sample of your daughter's cooking this way. Although if Belasko's word is true then we've nothing to fear on that account," said Prince Kellan. He coughed. "Now, would there be anything in the way of refreshment?"

Kander clasped his hands together. "Of course your highness, I have an excellent Cantrian red that I've been saving for a special occasion. Or would you prefer some of our beer? Brewed to my family's recipe."

"The beer is very good," Belasko said. "Definitely worth a try."

"I tell you what, good innkeeper, how about we each have a flagon of your beer to start and then wine with our meal?" said the king.

"Of course your majesty. Please, make yourselves comfortable. I'll bring the beer and then tell you the menu for the evening."

"Excellent. Oh, and Kander? Don't tell your daughter who your guests are. Not yet. We wouldn't want to put her off."

"Whatever's the matter, Father?" Kendra asked as Kander appeared in the kitchen. "You're sweating. Who's the swordsman brought with him to get you in such a state?"

Kander blinked at his daughter as he mopped his brow. "Oh, no one, no one... Just some important people from the palace. They've asked for some beer before dinner, which I'm to take them now. What have you cooked for them? Just so I can give them the menu."

Kendra gave her father a wicked grin. "Oh, I've something special for them. Plain, honest fair, the sort that they're probably crying out for at the palace. You can only take so many stuffed larks' tongues, you know."

"Wicked child, you'll be the death of me. You know this is your chance to impress these people. Important people."

Kendra frowned. "Yes, you've said. Well, Belasko praised my seasoning, which got me thinking. I'm making a deceptively plain menu, hearty but delicious. Just three courses. A country vegetable soup to start, venison stew for the main, poached pears for dessert."

Kander swallowed. "Very good, very good. I'll just take the beer up and let them know."

"You might as well pull on the Water King's beard as try to find a truly peaceful Baskan," Prince Kellan said. "Why? Because a peaceful Baskan no more exists than the bogeyman the common people say lives down by the docks."

His father sighed and shook his head at the mention of the mythical figure. "Well, with the trouble we've been having along the southern border I fear we may be heading towards war once more, despite out best efforts to come to peaceful terms in recent years."

Prince Kellan snorted. "Those bloody Baskan upstarts, they—"

"Are just doing what our own ancestors did, long ago," his sister interrupted. "Which you'd know if you'd paid attention to old Eade's history lessons."

"That pompous fart, how anyone could listen to him without falling asleep I don't know."

"You certainly did that often enough, otherwise you might have learned a thing or two."

King Mallor laughed. "Peace my children, peace. Kellan, Lilliana is quite right. Please, my dear, expand on the subject for your wayward brother." Kellan flushed as Lilliana continued.

"Thank you, Father. You see, brother, hundreds of years ago we were just like the Baskans. A young nation looking to expand, taking land and wealth from others. If we hadn't been as the Baskans are now, we would still be ruling over a small fortified settlement on the island where our palace stands. We never had much cause to worry about our neighbours to the south, a ragtag collection of squabbling city states and principalities too busy fighting amongst each other to cause us any bother. But then..."

"They stopped squabbling, and unified under one dominant house." King Mallor's face was grim now. "Unified whether they liked it or not. They've been a single nation for all of two generations and, as Lilliana says, started looking to expand. Which brought them into conflict with us in the Last War, in which Belasko here acquitted himself so well and helped keep the Baskans back."

Belasko inclined his head towards the king, accepting the compliment. "Thank you, your majesty, although it took the effort and lives of a great many men and women to push the Baskan forces back." He leaned forward, resting his elbows on the table. "I'm curious to know why you think we might be at risk of another war."

King Mallor frowned and began to speak, before pausing at a knock on the door, followed by Kander bustling in with a tray of beers in his hands. He set about serving them, placing the flagons on the table. The king reached out, picked up his flagon, and took a sip. He made an appreciative face. "My dear Kander, this is very fine indeed. Never mind your daughter working in the kitchens, could I induce you to come work in my brew house?"

Kander smiled. "That's very kind of your majesty. It's a family recipe, as I said, and I think it as fine a beer as you'll find."

"I'll drink to that," said Prince Kellan, raising his tankard in salute. He took a deep swallow and sighed, smacking his lips. "I swear, I think you might be right."

Princess Lilliana picked up her tankard and took a delicate sip. She smiled. "I don't drink much beer, but this really is a most pleasant flavour."

Belasko raised his own tankard. "Your health, your majesty, and yours, your highnesses — and to your prosperity, Kander." He took a sip and smiled at the innkeeper. "Now my friend, what are we having for dinner?"

The innkeeper cleared his throat. "Kendra has prepared a meal that is, in her own words, simple and hearty." He flushed. "According to her there are only so many stuffed larks' tongues a man can take."

Prince Kellan hooted with laughter. "By God, she's bold but she's not wrong."

The rest of the meal passed in good humour. Belasko and the royal guests praised the quality of the food in such terms that set Kander's ears to blazing, and at last, replete, they nursed full stomachs and glasses of brandy.

King Mallor sighed. "I say, Belasko, you were not wrong. That was as fine a meal as I've had in quite some time."

Prince Kellan took a large swig of brandy. "The innkeeper's got a good cellar too. Damn fine beer, followed by damn fine wines, and now a damn fine brandy."

The king scowled at his son. "Of course that would be what you took from this evening."

Prince Kellan returned his father's scowl. "And what is that supposed to mean?"

King Mallor gestured expansively with his brandy glass. "The entire repast we've just enjoyed — delicious, flavourful, perfectly seasoned, and yes, with well-matched drinks. An evening spent in intelligent conversation with good company, venturing out into the city beyond our usual rounds. And the thing you fixate on is the alcohol."

The prince shrugged, a sullen expression working its way across his face. "So? A man is allowed a few vices."

King Mallor snorted. "A few vices? There's precious few you *don't* have. When I was your age..."

*Oh dear, here we go.*

"When you were my age you were already king, and wed," snapped Prince Kellan. "If you want me to act responsibly then maybe you should give me some responsibilities, instead of hoarding everything for yourself."

A loud bang reverberated around the room as the king slammed his hand down on the table. "Responsibilities? If you acted responsibly in the first place..." His face reddened and his voice grew louder as he spoke.

"Your majesty, your highness, please," Belasko interjected, "let us not spoil an enjoyable evening. There is a place and a time for such arguments. Far be it for me to proscribe you, but I think that now may not be such."

Glowering at each other, tempers still simmering beneath the surface, the king and prince both settled back into their chairs. Lilliana toyed with the stem of her wine glass, avoiding eye contact. King Mallor forced a smile. "You are right, of course. As you so often are." His expression softened. "I'm sorry, son. I am quick to anger, but have only your best interests at heart."

Prince Kellan gave his own hesitant smile, before leaning forward and placing his hand on his father's. "I know, Father. Apologies. I have created a part for myself and sometimes I feel forced to play it. As you say, the food was exceptional tonight. I propose we offer this girl the position."

Mallor nodded, squeezing his son's hand in response. "I agree. Lilliana, what do you think?"

Princess Lilliana, who had remained silent through the outburst, gave a sad smile. "I think that it's a shame our dinners must so often end in argument — but the food was exquisite. We should definitely have this talent in the palace kitchens."

King Mallor nodded. "Agreed on all points. Belasko, could you send one of the guards to fetch Kander and his daughter — what is her name? Kendra?"

Belasko stood, pushing back his chair. "Of course, your majesty." He went to the door, opened it and murmured a few words to one of the guards outside, before closing it again and returning to the table. He poured all of them another measure of the brandy from the decanter that Kander had thoughtfully left on the table, before retaking his seat. Belasko raised his glass to the light before taking a sip. "You know," he murmured, "your highness is correct. This is damn fine brandy."

The king snorted, the prince and princess laughed, and there came a tap at the door.

"Enter," said the king.

Kander came in with Kendra close behind. She was muttering to herself about the arrogance of patrons bidding them enter in their own inn, when she laid eyes on their evening's guests. Those eyes went wide as saucers and she dropped into a deep curtsy. "Your majesty, your highnesses. I had no idea... I hope our poor table hasn't offended you." She stood back up, glaring at her father. "I'd have offered better if I knew who was dining with us."

King Mallor laughed. "Peace young lady, don't blame your father. I asked him to keep our presence a secret, and your table was far from poor. I can't remember the last time I had a meal as satisfying. You know, there really *is* such a thing as too many stuffed larks' tongues." Kendra blushed, shooting her father another look. The king cleared his throat. "However, you will still have to learn how to prepare such delicacies when you start work in the palace kitchens."

Kendra flushed. "When I... Do you mean to say — that is, your majesty — are you offering me a job?"

Princess Lilliana smiled. "He most certainly is. If you'll take it?"

Kendra nodded vigorously. "Yes, of course your highness, I'd be honoured. Oh, thank you! Thank you so much."

"Belasko will arrange the details, as well as providing adequate compensation for the meal we've enjoyed tonight. What do you think, a gold sovereign?"

Both Kander and Kendra gawped. "Your majesty," said the innkeeper, "that's far too generous..."

"Nonsense." The king dismissed his objection with a

wave of his hand. "I feel it is almost too little compensation for robbing you of such a fine cook. Now, if you wouldn't mind leaving us to finish our brandy, we won't take up too much more of your evening."

Once they'd shuffled out, offering effusive thanks, the four dining companions looked at each other.

"Well, Belasko," said the king, "that was well done."

"Thank you, your majesty. I know you like to see talent rewarded."

"Just as you hate to see it wasted. You were right, that young woman's skills deserve a chance to shine."

"Speaking of shining," Prince Kellan stood, draining his brandy glass. "I have a very bright possibility of an evening's entertainment to pursue. If you'll excuse me, Father?"

Mallor looked his son over before nodding his assent. "Thank you for coming with us, son. We should do things like this more often."

Kellan grinned at his father. "You won't find me arguing. Good night Father, good night Sister. Good night Belasko." He tipped them all a salute, picked up his cloak, and left. Lilliana also stood.

"If you'll forgive me Father, I feel the need for some fresh air after that brandy. Would you mind if I joined the guards outside before we return to the palace?"

"Of course not my dear one, we'll be just behind you."

Princess Lilliana smiled before putting on her cloak and making her way out of the room

King Mallor sighed, shaking his head.

"What is it, your majesty?" Belasko asked.

"I fear for my children, and for our people. If anything were to happen to me... If neither of my children marry and produce an heir soon then the line of succession isn't clear. Distant cousins and foreign powers that we're tied to by blood might make claim to the throne. There could be civil war as our country descends into the sort of squabbling behaviour for which we used to look down on our southern neighbours. And with added pressure from that southern quarter..." He shook his head again. "There's still time for both of them, but that son of mine... As much as I love him, I can't help but think he's not showing any signs of being ready for kingship."

"It is true that he enjoys himself, but—"

"Enjoys himself?" The king snorted. "He spends his evenings, every evening, carousing with wastrels. Drinking and whoring, in and out of the worst parts of the city. Between the two of us, I'm concerned that if he doesn't temper his behaviour then before long we'll have a royal bastard to contend with, if he hasn't fathered one already. Now Lilliana is a much more sober child. Behaves in a way suited to her station."

"I won't disagree with you sire, not to either of your children's merits or misfortunes. However, I think Kellan would surprise you, given the chance."

Mallor raised an eyebrow. "You do, do you?" A look flashed in his eyes, the message clear: *know your place.* King Mallor had done much to ease the stuffy formality of the court that he had inherited from his father, but even so Belasko's origins were not always easily overcome.

Belasko leaned forward in his chair. "I do. I think, if given more responsibility, he would show himself to be... Well, responsible. At heart he wants to please you, to impress. He only acts out in the way he does out of boredom, I'm sure of it. Give him something to do and I think he would rise to the challenge."

The king pursed his lips, thinking. Eventually he sighed. "You might be right, although I fear it may well be too late.

I'm loathe to offer him something until he's proven himself."

"How can he ever prove himself ready, if he's never given the opportunity?"

Mallor laughed at that, draining his own glass and making to rise. "Well said. Maybe you don't keep your brain in your scabbard after all."

## 2

The palace kitchens were a hot and busy place, a bustling network of rooms dedicated to preparing, producing, and preserving food for the royal household. There were multiple pantries and larders, kitchens full of ovens for baking, fireplaces for roasting, cooking pots and cauldrons bubbling away, all combining to make a fragrant and noisy workplace. It teemed with staff in their uniforms of white aprons embroidered with the royal sigil, worn over sturdy work clothes. Amongst all that, Kendra's new colleagues still managed to make themselves heard.

"Where did you say you worked before?"

Kendra sighed. They all knew she had worked at an inn, that she was a 'discovery', that Belasko had helped arrange her new job. The only reason they kept asking was to try and hammer home a point. *You do not belong. You shouldn't be here. You should go back to your inn and remember your place.*

*They* were a group of the other kitchen staff who had decided that she wasn't worthy to work in their august company, some younger than her, some older, but all with the same chip on their shoulder. Some of them were gathered around her now, while she worked to prepare their midday meal.

"The same place as when you last asked, Tarvin."

Tarvin grinned. He was a lanky youth who had taken to picking on her. Other staff had gathered around, letting Tarvin do the talking while they sniggered up their sleeves. "Oh yes, your family inn, wasn't it? How was it you managed to get a job here again? It's quite a jump from an inn in one of the, um, *lesser* parts of town, to the palace kitchens."

Kendra sighed again, before using a long spoon to taste the stew she was preparing. She nodded to herself, satisfied. "You know the answer to that question, too. You ask it often enough." A few of the other staff laughed at that. Perhaps she was winning a few of them over. "You'll see what kind of cook I am in a few minutes, if you can stop talking long enough to put something in your mouth."

"Oh," Tarvin murmured under his breath, moving closer, "I'm sure I can stop talking long enough for something..."

The other staff had gone silent, uncomfortable at the turn that events had taken. Tarvin reached out a hand to grab hold of her but stopped short, a look of surprise on his face.

Kendra laughed. "That's right, look down why don't you?" Tarvin did as she bid, wincing at the extremely sharp kitchen knife she held to his crotch, catching at the material of his apron and pressing into the clothes and flesh beneath. "Did I tell you my father was a soldier? He taught me to look after myself. Remember that the next time you try to lay hands on me, or you might end up missing some essential equipment."

Tarvin had gone white as a sheet. Trembling, he backed

away. From a safe distance he gathered himself, then spat at her feet. "That's for you, whore. As if I would even want to touch you." With that he stalked off, alone. His acolytes decided not to follow and dispersed to their own places in the kitchens.

*How long will it be like this?* Kendra thought to herself. *Two weeks now, and still the other staff don't warm to me. I didn't think it would be like this.*

Later that day Belasko came to visit her. She was preparing a dessert, when a voice at her elbow surprised her.

"Settling in okay?"

She whirled around, clutching a wooden spoon. When she saw who it was she relaxed and smiled. "Oh Belasko, sorry, you made me jump. Yes, well enough, thank you. I'm actually cooking for the royal table now."

The king's champion nodded, looking around the room. "Everyone treating you alright?"

"Mostly, yes."

"Mostly? Some haven't? Let me guess: that lanky string of piss is one of them?" He nodded towards the far corner, where Tarvin was taking a tray of cakes out of one of the big ovens. He had been glaring at them but, surprised at being noticed, he became very interested in his work.

Kendra laughed. "Yes. A few of them have been unpleasant, Tarvin there chief among them. They seem to think they're above a cook from a humble inn."

Belasko snorted. "Some people born into below-stairs families seem to think they have the standing of their above-stairs masters. Ridiculous. We're all working people. Why should it matter where you're from? It should be about what you can do."

He was frowning now. She studied him for a moment, taking in the broad shoulders that tapered to a narrow waist, the averagely handsome face. He wasn't overly tall, but carried himself well. He walked into any room like he was taking command of it, and there was a steady confidence to him that she liked. Belasko was dressed for travelling, a woollen cloak over a black, fitted jacket chased with silver embroidery, white shirt peeking through at the collar. He wore sturdy breeches over his stockings and knee-high riding boots. Blushing, she realised that her moment of observation had stretched a little long. "It's alright. Pellero, the head chef, has taken a liking to me — or rather, to my food."

Belasko laughed. "Oh, that old rogue. Yes, he'll like you well enough as long as you keep him fed. What are you making there?"

She gestured to her workstation. "Poached pears, the same as I made when you brought the king and prince to our inn. They seem to have become the prince's favourite dessert, he wants them every evening. I'm making them just for him tonight — everyone else is having something different."

"Good, I'm glad. Unfortunately I won't get to see him enjoy them. I was due to dine at the royal table, but I've been called away to the Academy on business. I'll be back soon, in a few days. Let me know if you have any more trouble with the other staff. I can't stand bullies."

"I will, thank you. And thank you for coming by as well, I owe you for helping get me this position. I won't forget it."

He smiled. "That's quite alright. I like to see talent rewarded. I'll see you again soon." Belasko left, exchanging a few words with some of the other staff on his way out. He waved to Pellero, who was observing the kitchen from a stool in the centre of the room, before ducking out the door.

A short while later there was another visitor to the kitchen, a man dressed in the black of the inquisition. The presence of one of the king's own investigators, those tasked with rooting out threats to the crown, could dampen any atmosphere. The general hubbub of the kitchen subsided as he knocked at the door and waited until one of the staff could attend to him. Pellero himself lumbered over and a few words were exchanged before the head chef nodded and pointed Kendra out. The inquisitor looked over and she met his eyes — or rather, eye. With a start she realised he had only one, his left eye covered with a black patch. The inquisitor nodded at her, then beckoned her over with a crooked finger. Kendra swallowed around a lump that felt lodged in her throat.

"Hey," she called to Allana, the cook working nearest to her. "Can you keep an eye on this please? Make sure it doesn't boil over?" Allana's eyes flicked up from her own work to meet Kendra's gaze only briefly. She nodded, otherwise expressionless. "Thank you!" Kendra said, before leaving her work station and making her way over to the door.

She curtsied when she got close to the inquisitor. "Hello sir, how can I help?" she said as she straightened.

He looked down at her, a tall man with a shock of sandy hair, face unreadable. He may have been clad in the black of the Inquisition, but the fine detailing and tailoring on his jacket marked him out as a man of rank as much as did the golden sun and twin stars picked out on his shoulder. Clearly a man that took pride in his appearance, he was immaculately turned out. The collar and cuffs of his shirt neatly pressed into crisp lines, boots polished until they shone, golden jacket buttons gleaming. He attempted a smile but it didn't seem like an expression with which his face was familiar. "Just a few questions Miss, routine when someone starts in a position close to the royal family. It should have been attended to before. My apologies for disrupting your work."

She returned his unsure smile with a warmer one of her own. "That's alright sir, ask me anything you like."

"Thank you." He took out a small sheaf of papers and a charcoal pencil from a pouch at his belt. "First of all, your name?"

"Kendra, sir."

He nodded, jotting as he went. "And were you born here in the city?"

"Yes, sir."

"Father's name and occupation?"

"Kander sir, an innkeeper."

"An inn in the city?"

"Yes sir, the Golden Hind, over by the fourth gate."

The inquisitor nodded. "I know it. Not the best part of town, but the inn has a good reputation. Your mother?

"Dead, sir."

He grimaced. "My condolences."

"That's alright, it's been a long time."

The inquisitor nodded. "Well, an old grief can still sting. Are you married?"

"I was, sir. My husband died in the sweating sickness that came through our neighbourhood a few years back. It's just me and my boy now."

"I'm sorry, a lot of people lost family in that illness. You say you have a son; how old is he?"

"Five years. My father cares for him while I'm working in the kitchens, with some help. He's a sweet-natured boy, but always falling into mischief. "

The inquisitor gave a more genuine smile this time. "That is, I understand, the nature of small children." He tucked away his sheaf of papers and pencil and gave her a nod. "That's all I need. Again, I'm sorry to disturb. What is it I've taken you away from?"

"I'm making poached pears for the prince's dessert. They seem to have become his favourite."

"Well then, far be it for me to keep our good prince from his dessert. Good evening, Mistress Kendra."

"And to you, sir."

The inquisitor gave her a shallow bow, then turned and was on his way.

Kendra went to go back to her work and frowned. Tarvin was walking away from her work station. What was he doing there? She walked back, looking over her things and inspecting the pears, but nothing seemed to be amiss. Kendra looked over at Allana, who had been keeping an eye on her station but she was absorbed in her own work. She looked over at Tarvin but he avoided her gaze, keeping his attention on what he was doing. She inspected the dessert she had been working on. Taking a very small spoonful of the sauce and a slim sliver of flesh from one of the pears, Kendra raised them to her nose. She sniffed them and, having detected nothing out of the ordinary, tentatively tasted. Both seemed fine. Kendra shrugged. Whatever mischief was on the boy's mind, he clearly hadn't managed to carry it out.

The rest of the meal preparation passed quietly, for the

most part. A member of the Baskan ambassador's staff appeared as they were putting the finishing touches on the evening meal. He gave Pellero strict instructions regarding a traditional Baskan dish that was due to be served at a reception in a few days' time. A small, thin, balding man with a stony face, he insisted on a tour of the kitchens. Remarking all the while on the differences between the kitchen at the royal palace in the Baskan capital, not all of them favourable, he then left.

It was later that evening, as she cleaned down her countertop, that Kendra became aware of a commotion from the service end of the kitchen. There were screams and shouting, and then three guardsmen burst through the service doors into the kitchen.

"No one leave!" shouted the first guard, a grim look on his face. "The prince is dead. Murdered. No one is allowed to leave."

Kendra looked around her, taking in a view that had not changed for the last few hours. She was terrified, her surroundings giving her nothing to do but contemplate her fate. To make matters worse she had been violently ill, several times, and was now shivering uncontrollably. She and the rest of the kitchen staff had been escorted down to the palace dungeons, in the basement of one of the palace's far-flung towers. They had been separated and placed into solitary cells, presumably so they couldn't confer over the shocking events of the day.

*Prince Kellan dead,* Kendra thought to herself. *I can't believe it. I know some thought ill of him, but he seemed so nice.*

Her cell was small, the ceiling only just high enough for

her to stand up. A rough pallet along one wall and a filthy bucket were her only comforts. A small grate up near the ceiling would presumably let in some light during the day, though it was fully dark now. As summer was now ended and the longer nights of autumn were drawing in, this grate would let in less and less light over time. One wall was made entirely of bars, granting her no privacy from outside observers. A portion of this wall was a locked gate that swung inward when opened. Hers was just one in a line of cells along the corridor, the furthest from the entrance, although none of the other cells seemed to be occupied. The atmosphere was damp and cold, smelling of mould, her own vomit, and more unpleasant things.

*I wonder what time it is? It must be hours since dinner service.*

The only light came from some crude torches in wall sconces along the corridor. They emitted an unpleasant black smoke and the light they cast was faltering and sickly, matching Kendra's feelings perfectly.

There came an echo of footsteps from down the corridor, drawing nearer. Kendra tried to stand up straight, chin up, determined to meet whoever came as boldly as she could. But she found herself swaying slightly, shivering with whatever ague had hold of her. The footsteps slowed as they approached, until a figure appeared in front of her cell. It was the one-eyed inquisitor she had spoken to earlier that day. He slowed to a stop outside her cell, regarding her in silence for a long moment. When he cleared his throat it made her jump.

"Mistress Kendra. I didn't expect to see you again so soon."

"Nor I you, sir."

"No. I'm sure you would have no reason to expect to see

me again. None at all." He reached into a shadowed alcove in the wall behind him, pulling out a short three-legged stool on which he sat in silence, looking at her.

Kendra broke the silence first. "Sir, is it true? What the guards said? Is the prince... dead?"

He nodded slowly. "I'm afraid so. It is a dark day."

"Oh, Aronos, lord of all, preserve him, the poor man." Kendra found that her hands were shaking and clutched them together. "A dark day indeed. Evil, even."

The inquisitor had noticed her hands. "Ah dear Kendra, is it too cold in here for you? Or is it something else? Are you scared?"

"Of course I'm scared," Kendra blurted. "The prince is dead and all of the kitchen staff have been dragged off into cells. It's cold in here, I feel sick, and I'm worried for my son. They will have expected me home hours ago."

He nodded slowly, deliberately. "Well, it seems like the prince was poisoned. Something slipped into his dinner. Surely you can see we had to round up the kitchen staff?"

"Poisoned? Oh, dear god..."

"I'm afraid so. As to the condition of your accommodation, well..." The inquisitor waved his hands vaguely to indicate her cell. "Where else would you put people you needed to question? Now, your family. I will send a note to your father at the Golden Hind to let him know that you're helping us with our enquiries. Alright?"

Kendra nodded, smiling weakly. "Thank you sir, that is most kind."

He waved away her thanks. "Not at all, it's the least I can do. After all, I'm sure you're going to be very helpful, aren't you?"

"Yes sir, I'll do all that I can to help."

"Good, good. That's... good." The inquisitor relaxed on

his stool, leaning back to rest against the wall. He crossed one leg over the other, idly tapping on one of his boots with a fingernail. "I'm sure you can be helpful to us. It's to do with the food the prince ate this evening. We're trying to narrow down the source of his poisoning and we've discovered that this evening the prince ate exactly the same food as everyone else. Except for one thing." He paused, watching her expectantly. There was silence, apart from the tap-tap-tap of his fingernail on his boot.

Eventually Kendra spoke. "It was the pears, wasn't it? The ones I prepared. They were the only thing the prince had that was different to everyone else."

The inquisitor leaned forwards. "Yes, that's right. I believe you prepared them for him specially?"

Belasko was nearly ready to set off on the journey to the Academy, which was housed on his land outside the city, when a detachment of the palace guards rode into the courtyard of his city house, horseshoes ringing off the flagstones. They wore the black and gold of the royal house, a silver stag embroidered on their surcoats, and pulled up with a clatter of armour, surrounding him and his travelling companions. There was quite a crowd in the courtyard already, Belasko's staff having just finished the preparations for departure and loading up the pack horses. Orren, his long-time companion and manager of the Academy, put one hand to the blade at his waist. The air was thick with tension.

Belasko held up a hand. "Peace, friends! We'll find no trouble from the palace guard, I'm sure. Still your hands. We don't want anyone getting excited."

Orren gave him a flat look before reluctantly taking his hand from his sword hilt. Belasko had yet to mount, so led his horse by the reins, walking up to the woman who seemed to be leading the troops.

"Hello there. Do you command these guards? Hang on — is that Majel? Difficult to see in this light." It was getting darker, although sunset was still a while off and the lanterns were unlit in the courtyard.

A sharp-featured young woman with a fierce expression and her dark hair cut short, the rider sat up straight in her saddle. "It is, sir. And yes, I command these troops."

"Good to see you, it's been a while. Still practising those drills I gave you?" Belasko reached up and clasped the young commander's hand, giving it a firm shake.

"That I am sir, and I think I've seen some improvement. It's good to see you too, although I wish the circumstances were different."

Belasko leaned back, taking in the tension the riders showed for the first time. "Why, what are the circumstances?"

Majel swallowed. "I'm sorry to say we've been sent to escort you back to the palace. You're needed there."

Belasko nodded. "Of course, that's no problem. Are my people free to return to the Academy? They're due back this evening and their families will worry otherwise."

"My orders are only for you, sir. They are free to carry on their way."

"Thank you, Majel." Belasko spoke to his people. "Alright, you carry on home. Orren, remember what we said about the east pasture. I think we need to put in some sort of drainage there. Can you look into it and we'll make a decision when I'm back?"

Orren nodded, his shaggy blonde hair swaying.

"Alright. Make sure you come back when you can. There's decisions need making before winter that are above my station."

Belasko laughed. "Nonsense, you run the place so well I swear I'm hardly needed. Off you go now, I'll be safe in Majel's hands. Fare thee well."

Orren nodded again, raising a hand in salute to his friend and master, then to the young commander, and set heels to his horse's flanks. The others that rode with him clattered off behind, calling out their own farewells. As they disappeared through the gates, Belasko mounted his own horse and turned to Majel. "Shall we?" They set off down the wide cobbled road, the troops falling in behind as Belasko's household staff closed the courtyard gates.

Belasko looked at the young commander. "How long has it been now since you were at the Academy. Four years?"

Majel smiled. "Five, sir."

Belasko nodded. "Is it really? You seem to be doing well for yourself. You were a good student, you know."

"I had a good teacher."

They rode on in silence for several minutes.

"Majel," Belasko said, "what's really going on? Why am I needed at the palace?"

Majel looked down, muttering something under her breath. Belasko leaned closer to her. "What was that? I couldn't quite catch it." He was surprised to see tears in the eyes of his former student when she looked back up.

"Damn it," Majel said. "They didn't want me to tell you. But how can I not?"

"Tell me what?"

Majel cleared her throat, looking away when she spoke. "It's Prince Kellan. He's... he's dead."

Belasko felt the bottom of his stomach drop away, as if a

pit had just opened up inside him. "No," he whispered, "that can't be."

Majel turned back to him, angry now as much as upset. "It shouldn't be, but it can and it is."

"What happened? Some kind of accident? I saw him myself only earlier today."

"Poison." Majel spat the word, face wrinkling in disgust.

"How? The palace is the most secure building in Villan. How could he be poisoned?"

Majel shook her head. "I don't know. But that is what the inquisition are going to find out."

Kendra stared at the inquisitor in shock. "That's... that's impossible. I prepared the pears myself. No one else went near them."

The inquisitor met her gaze. "Well, that's a problem then, isn't it? Are you saying that you poisoned the prince?"

Kendra felt the blood drain from her face. "Me? No, I-I wouldn't, I didn't, I couldn't do that!"

He nodded. "I'm sure. Where would a humble cook procure poison in the first place? Particularly one that must have been expensive, being undetectable in the food either by taste or scent. A rare poison indeed, requiring deeper pockets than you possess. Are you sure that no one else went near the dish during preparation?"

Kendra's mind raced. "I can't think of anyone — wait! After we had our conversation earlier today I saw Tarvin, one of the other kitchen staff, walking away from my station. Allana was watching my station, but could he have slipped something into the food?"

The inquisitor shrugged. "I don't think so, I had my eye

on him while we talked." He smiled, tapping his eye patch with his forefinger. "Forgive my attempt at humour. I was watching him and didn't see him interfere with the food you were preparing. I have already spoken to Tarvin and he confessed that he intended to spoil it, as a prank, but was put off by my presence and didn't carry it out. Are you sure there was no one else? No other visitors today? Anything out of the ordinary?"

Kendra put her head in her hands, thinking, desperate to find a clue that would help prove her own innocence. She looked up.

"We had a visit from one of the Baskan ambassador's staff, bringing Pellero instructions for a Baskan dish that was due to be served at a reception this week."

Ervan raised his eyebrows. "Really? Now that is interesting. Do you remember if they passed by your work station at all?"

Kendra frowned, then shook her head. "No. He toured the kitchen but I don't remember him coming close to where I was working."

"Hmm... Can you describe him for me?"

"Middle aged, thin, balding. Face like a stone."

Ervan nodded. "Thank you. I'll add it to my notes and see if someone can pay the ambassadorial residence a visit. Now, were there any other visitors today? Anyone that came to your station, could have interfered with your work."

Something occurred to Kendra then: a thought, albeit an unpleasant one. She swallowed before she spoke. "There was one other. One other visitor today."

The inquisitor arched an eyebrow. "Oh? Who was that?"

Kendra shook her head. "But I'm sure it couldn't be, it's not possible..."

"I'll decide what's possible. You just tell me who came to visit you."

Kendra struggled to get the words out, tears coming. "Belasko. He-he came to visit me. To-to see how I was getting on."

"I see. Was the dish you were preparing left unattended at any point when he was with you, or were you distracted at all?"

"No, not left unattended. But-but I did look away once or twice, just for a moment. I'm sure it wasn't possible for him to — I mean, I just looked away for the briefest moment..." Her shoulders were shaking as she sobbed.

"There, there. I know it's upsetting. It's been an upsetting day for us all." He leaned forwards on his stool. "You think it was too short a time for him to have slipped something into the food, but I've seen Belasko fight." He tapped his eye patch again. "Before I lost this, when my vision was good. I know what his reflexes are like. The man can move quicker than a striking snake when he needs to. If anyone could have done it in a moment's distraction, it is Belasko."

Kendra tried to bring her sobs under control. "But he's loyal to the king, and the prince was his friend. Everyone knows that. Why would he do something like that?"

"That," said the inquisitor, "is for me to find out. We've sent men after Belasko, to bring him back to the palace."

"You've already sent men for him? But I only just told you that he came to the kitchens."

"Oh, I already knew that. I just wanted to see if you would tell me." The inquisitor stood, replacing his stool in the alcove. "Now, you said you've been sick. How are you feeling now? Achy, nauseas, shivery?" Kendra nodded. "Did you taste any of the dessert you were making?"

Again, Kendra nodded. "After I saw Tarvin near my

station, I tasted a little of the sauce. A small slice of pear. I couldn't see or smell anything wrong with the dish, I just wanted to make sure he hadn't tampered with it." Another bout of shivering struck her.

Ervan sighed. "Then you have taken a small dose of the poison that killed the prince. I will arrange a draught from the royal physician that should help." He smiled at her, the expression not reaching his eye. "You really have been most helpful. I'll see to that note for your family, and someone to fetch you some blankets and a brazier. You might be here a while." He turned and walked away, and Kendra was left alone with only the flickering torchlight and the echo of his footsteps for company.

The cell door slammed shut behind Belasko. *I should have known something was off when they asked for my sword at the gate. 'Precautions' my arse.*

It had been an embarrassing moment, for him and the guards. Majel had held her hand out, not meeting his eyes. "I'm sorry sir, I have my orders. None but the palace guard are to go armed within the walls until further notice."

Belasko had paused, reluctant to hand over his sword. He had not gone without a weapon in a long time. "I understand, although asking the king's champion to go unarmed when it is the royal family that has been harmed seems a little foolish to me."

Majel sighed. "To me too, but still..."

"Orders are orders. I understand. Here." He unbuckled his sword belt and handed it and his rapier to the young commander. "Look after this for me. At least then I know it's in good hands."

Majel swallowed as she took the weight of Belasko's blade. "Of course, sir. It'll be a privilege. Belasko. I, um, I need to escort you in now."

"Of course. Where are we going? To the royal chambers? I would like to see the king and whoever is leading the investigation."

"Well, the latter won't be a problem. They've asked to see you right away. I'm to take you now, to wait for them."

"Where are we going?"

Majel looked ashamed as she spoke. "To the dungeons, sir. They want to speak to you there."

"The dungeons. Majel? What's going on?"

"I don't know, sir. I'm sure it's all some mistake. Just come with me. The sooner they talk to you, the sooner this will all be sorted out."

Belasko let his former student lead him to the dungeons and place him in a cell, an uneasy feeling building as he went. Little did he know it, but his cell was the twin of Kendra's, right down to the damp and mouldy air. He turned as the door closed behind him.

"Shouldn't I be in chains? The imagery would certainly suit the venue, don't you think?"

Majel shifted from one foot to the other, shamefaced. *Poor woman. It's not her fault.* "Sorry, I know you are only doing your duty. Go tell whoever it is that wants to see me that I'm here and we can get this farce over with."

Majel nodded, turned and left. Hours passed and Belasko waited. And waited. There was no sign of anyone coming to question him. Finally his impatience got the better of him and he started to call out.

"Come on! I've been waiting for hours. Is there anyone there? This is ridiculous!" He called and shouted, banging on the bars of his cell, rattling the door in its hinges.

Eventually he heard footsteps approaching. He quieted himself, waiting to see who would appear. A figure emerged out of the gloom, dressed head-to-toe in black. *The Inquisition, then. That makes sense,* Belasko thought to himself, although he still felt a shiver run through him at the thought of being at the mercies of a member of that institution. Originally a semi-religious order created to bend people's worship to Aronos, the Sun God, and away from their old pagan ways, one of the king's ancestors had turned them into a not-so-secret police force. They had a terrifying reputation and it was considered best to avoid their notice. As they drew closer the figure's face became clear: a man with a shock of sandy hair, one eye covered by a patch. *The face is familiar...*

The inquisitor stopped outside his cell, looking him up and down. "Sorry," he said at last. "Busy night."

"I'm sure," said Belasko, "but what am I doing in the cells? Let me help you. I'm sure I can assist the investigation. I need to see the king, the poor man. Is the palace locked down, no one in or out since..." Belasko stopped, unable to say the words.

"Since the prince was poisoned at his own table? Yes, we do know what we're doing, thank you. As for seeing the king, I'm afraid that's impossible. He's quite distraught, as I'm sure you understand."

"Yes, of course. I just wish to bring what comfort I can."

"That would be precious little, being the source of at least some of his present misery."

Belasko blinked. "What? How?"

The inquisitor sighed. "Not only has his son just been murdered, but to find out that he has been betrayed by someone who was trusted above all others..."

Belasko felt suddenly cold all over, as if he had been

pushed into an icy lake. He struggled to get his breath. "What... what are you saying?"

The inquisitor smirked. "Just that a rather incriminating letter was found in the king's apartments this evening. That and other evidence gathered tonight means that you, Belasko, king's champion, are the foremost suspect in the murder of our prince."

Belasko could only stare at the man in black, who shrugged again. "I'm sure you will protest your innocence, but the evidence is rather stacking up against you. You'll have a chance to answer my questions tomorrow. Try to get some rest, if you can. It's been a long day."

"No," Belasko said as the inquisitor turned and walked away. "It's not true. It's not possible. The king can't believe that. He knows me too well, knows I love him and Kellan both. He must know I would never..." He was at the bars to his cell now, shouting between them at the retreating back of the inquisitor. "I would never hurt the prince. I'm innocent! Please, send for the king. I must see the king!"

The inquisitor, unmoved, faded into implacable shadow as Belasko slumped against the bars of his cell.

*It can't be. It just can't be.*

# AFTERWORD

*The Swordsman's Intent* is a prequel novella to my novel *The Swordsman's Lament*, which is set 15 years later. If you've read this far then you've already read the sample chapters included with this book. I hope you enjoyed them.

If you liked this adventure and would like to be kept up to date with my news (as well as receiving free short stories and exclusive content) then make sure to sign up to my newsletter at https://gmwhite.co.uk/tsi-landing-page/.

Authors live and die by their reviews, so if you've enjoyed *The Swordsman's Intent*, please consider leaving a review at the retailer where you purchased the book (or on Goodreads). Even a line or two would be incredibly helpful and it would mean the world to me.

# BY THE AUTHOR

The Royal Champion Series:
Prequel Novella: The Swordsman's Intent
Book One: The Swordsman's Lament
Book Two: The Swordsman's Descent

# ABOUT THE AUTHOR

G.M. White has always been an avid reader, a love of the written word instilled in him by his parents at an early age. This may or may not have something to do with the fact that he was a very talkative child and the only time he was quiet was when he had his head in a book. Anyway, we'll give them the benefit of the doubt on that one.

A lifelong storyteller, he finally decided to put his imagination to good use and set pen to paper (well, fingers to keyboard) and started to write down the worlds that he carried with him in his head. His first novel, *The Swordsman's Lament*, was published in 2019.

A reformed Londoner, he now lives on St Martin's in the Isles of Scilly.